W9-ADC-597

Tree of Heaven

Tree of Heaven

R.C. Binstock

William Butler Yeats'
"He wishes his Beloved were Dead"
from
The Wind Among The Reeds (1899)

Published by
Soho Press, Inc.
853 Broadway
New York, NY 10003

Library of Congress Cataloging-in-Publication Data

Binstock, R. C., 1958–
Tree of heaven / R. C. Binstock.
p. cm.
ISBN 1-56947-038-3
1. China—History—1937–1945—Fiction. I. Title.
PS3552.I573T74 1995
813'.54—dc20 94-41552
CIP

Book design and composition by
The Sarabande Press

For Esther, my daughter

EASTERN ANHWEI PROVINCE

EAST-CENTRAL CHINA

FEBRUARY 1938

If our country is subjugated by the enemy, we shall lose everything. We cannot even speak of socialism if we are robbed of a country in which to practice it.

—MAO TSE-TUNG

We played with the daughter as we would with a harlot. As the parents kept insisting that their daughter should be returned to them, we killed the mother and father. We then played with the daughter again as before, until our unit marched on, when we killed her.

—JAPANESE SOLDIER IN CHINA,
LETTER HOME

FIRE

ONE

Suzuki was here again today, just after luncheon. He says we will certainly leave in the morning or at the latest on Wednesday. For weeks we have been motionless; for days we have been waiting for the order to depart. Still there is delay. Not that any notice is ever given, or explanation—it is not that sort of army—but by now we are confounded by their mystery and deceit. My own suspicion grows and grows. Even if I do not question the authority of our leaders, or their skill, I must question their intent; this is not simple conquest. They mean to achieve victory here but also something else, something larger. Something that will bring them a kind of triumph over their own people, a kind they have never had before.

Suzuki, with his offensive braying laugh, was as always

hinting that he knows more than he reveals. He is only a major and a somewhat unimpressive one. I believe he was in training as a schoolteacher before he entered the Academy and I think he must be of an influential family, else he could not have been commissioned at all, or have risen so high. If generals confide in the likes of him I am very surprised. But I fear him. I fear him because I am unsure of his friends; I fear him because he is my superior officer. I fear him because I do not know why I am here, and I suspect that he does.

He insisted on sitting down at my small table with me, though it had not yet been cleared, though I was plainly reading a letter from home. It was a letter from my wife that I have now read over at least ten times because I find it oddly distant. As if the experiences of the last year have spun a curtain between us, a veil. Somehow I feel as if she is the one in the foreign land, while I sew and wait for her return; when she writes to me of this neighbor or that shopkeeper, people she implies I should well remember, I ask, why does she expect me to know these strangers? So what if she talked to such and such a person on the road? This has nothing to do with me. I live among these dark and muddy plains and hills.

With Suzuki staring directly at me and at the letter I had to fold it and return it to my pocket. I had risen to salute him and he carelessly indicated that I should regain my seat as he took the chair across from me. I asked if he had eaten and offered to have the orderly serve him but he laughed, horribly, and waved me off. He took out a cigarette and I lit it for him and then we sat, as he smoked and looked out over the camp and I surveyed the slowly drying scraps of food on the dishes before me.

This morning I saw further evidence of a disturbing

trend. There are a good many more Chinese women around the camp now, young and healthy women who are plainly under the protection of particular officers, and considered their property. They are always working hard and bear expressions of intense fear but it is chronic fear, not a terror of the moment, and if they are not well dressed they have at least enough clothing to cover their bodies and protect them from the cold, and they are clean and whole, which is not typically the case with the Chinese around the camp, or in fact anywhere that the Emperor's Army has been in this country. One might think that with all the women of this huge nation freely available to them, with no civil institution or law to stand in their way, these criminals would not bother to associate themselves with any individual victim; one might think they would continue to take and discard as they chose. But the officers are different from the men, of course, with impulses beyond the animal, and may well experience some small desire to be as they once were. Every person wants order; even the most savage feel the need, at times, for kindness and affection, or whatever passes for it in the darknesses of their minds, and I assume one can purchase much affection, from a Chinese, with the coin of food and warmth, and security of life and limb. I have no doubt that the women are very amorous in their attentions despite their fright and the devastation of their homeland. It is a degradation that sickens me, but it is human and unsurprising. I have seen much worse.

Suzuki, after telling me what he claims to know about our movements and refusing to share with me the reasons for the delay, wanted to talk about physics. Of all things. Perhaps he was first in the science class at his high school in a southern prefecture in 1912 and cultivates an interest in ideas as a consequence. Perhaps his guilt and his uncertainty play tricks with his heart. At any rate he is aware that I am a scientist and botany and physics are all the same to him, and he wanted to talk about the German thinker Einstein and his energy-matter equation. It was a very odd topic to raise in the chilly noonday sun, sitting before my tent on the hillside in this vast camp on this enormous rising plain, but it struck him as perfectly normal and chatty. I know very little about these sorts of things (I am astonished that Suzuki even knows who Einstein is) but I understand the principle well enough, which he seems also to do; I was unclear about what he wanted from me. He asked if I believed that all the lights of the world could be lit and all the trains powered and the factories run by the energy released from a single stone, and I said that if the theories were correct then that indeed was the case. He asked if I thought we would see such a development—the total release of the energy in matter—within our lifetimes. I have become very cautious and so gave the answer I would have given, in sincerity, five years ago or more: that with the progress made of late by our culture and our institutions of learning, nothing would surprise me. He looked me in the eye and asked me if I truly believed it would happen. As he watched me I remembered the conviction I have so often had during the chaos of the recent past—that despite my detestation for him, Suzuki is the only human being in my universe who understands that my soul is crying out in horror—and I answered him honestly: no. He asked if perhaps I thought it just as well. When I waited for him to explain he gestured broadly to the army around us and asked what the men would do if there were no need of their labor. This is not labor, I wanted to say, but held my tongue. Suzuki has a heart, at least a small and torpid one, but he is no friend of mine.

It is not that I find the deaths of all these Chinese, per se, to be such a great loss; there are far too many of them and everybody knows it. It is not that I have respect for these people, or find them equal to the Japanese. Of course they are not. The level of education here is abysmal, the exploitation of one by another constant and appalling, the living conditions of the large majority unacceptable and entirely uncivilized even before we arrived. We cannot possibly cause them more suffering than they have continually caused themselves. I have, in fact, seen no evidence at all of the superiority the Chinese have always claimed; I am not even sure if I have yet seen one truly intelligent face. Our own society is not perfect but they have much to learn from us, and we little from them.

Unfortunately—tragically—they are being taught nothing but how un-Japanese the Japanese can become when let outside the strictures of their native towns and villages. What an example this is; what an impression we are making! It is as if the very worst moments, the deepest failures of will, of all the lives of all the residents of all the islands of Japan have been collected and purified and instilled into one million strong, heedless young men, set loose where no one will see what they do, where no one will care. It is as if we have been abandoned, abruptly, by our ancestors, because we left our homes and crossed over the sea.

When Suzuki had gone I went into my tent and tried to answer my wife's letter. After twenty minutes of effort I gave that up and lay instead on my cot, remembering a few of the events I have been party to and attempting to order my recollections into some sort of sequence. I have always prided myself on knowing exactly what happened when and where and it bothers me terribly that I have become so confused. In another twenty minutes I was not confused but sleepy, and before I knew it I had lost consciousness entirely.

For many of us sleep is most tempting of all. There is little entertainment here, little distraction. If one is not a sadist or a killer there is nothing to excite the mind or the senses, nothing at all, and even sadists and killers must escape themselves now and then. In a military way there is not much to do because there are no longer any Chinese soldiers to fight, or living prisoners to be guarded, and no pretense of exercising control over the men; so long as they show proper deference to us we do not care how they behave. I should correct myself, for I suppose that is not true. Most of the officers still care, I imagine. Order is all, appearance is all, and it is not easy to discard an entire way of life. But I do not care—I once did, but no longer—and I have much to forget and little to do. There is nothing I can use to nurture serenity but sleep.

We are resting on the outskirts; now the battles are elsewhere. We have waited here for weeks, ready to leave when they tell us. Waiting is exhausting but I will wait carefully and expertly, because it is required of me. It is the reason I am here. I wonder where the others are, the other fighters, the other armies. I wonder if it is the same for them this day, this week, this year: empty conquest of a hollow land and endless waiting in the cold and bitter wind. But I am only myself; I can pitch my tent in just one place. At this moment it is on the plain, but I will be ready when the order is given, and I will go.

TWO

I want not to feel. I cannot possibly say how the earth can have come to this state, but I want to feel nothing about it. I want not to know but that is impossible. Failing ignorance I seek numbness. I seek coldness and hardness. I want not to care. I am far from home and among strangers and even in better times they would find me grave and unapproachable, surely, and queer, because of my fear of them, the fear I have always supported through distance, but now I am not afraid. The worst has come (or if not the worst, the worst I can imagine; there may yet be worse and if so that will be the new worst in its time) and there is nothing left to be frightened by. I want not to fear and that has finally been accomplished. Soon I will be left without feelings entirely.

I want not to be responsible. I want to live another day.

I do not want to feel lucky, or to guess the odds. I want to breathe one moment and then again the next, to not hurt, to stay warm and dry. I want not to be self-conscious, not to be required. I am in motion. This is just another day.

These are the ruins of my country. I am the remnant of its horror. If I were free I could start walking from this spot and walk for miles and pass the looted farms and the burning villages, pass the graves of hundreds of brothers and sisters and uncles and aunts, thousands, who would demand gratitude for my survival, for my deliverance from their fate, and also many more still living but savaged, who might well ask the same. I would not offend them by correcting them—I would not offend the dead—but my concern is not for myself alone. I wish not to feel for them as I wish not to feel for myself, more urgently in truth. I seek to escape the calculation of grief. All my life I was happy for my modest wealth and comfort; it was almost a habit. I understood my own good fortune. But now if I am grateful for the fact that I have not been shot or beaten or violated I must be sorrowful for them, and this is what I cannot do. I cannot do this and continue to care for myself, to remain intact through each hour. The only thing I can do for them is to survive, and in the act I must refuse them, I must become the cruel stone woman they have always believed me to be. I must do this for myself and as the invaders respect cruelty—more than that they are attached to it, they worship it, it is the blood of their humanity, the image in their eye—I am pleased to have some practice, some knowledge of the art. But I am largely a novice and I regret this; I've had no opportunity, in the past, to steal or to punish, to damage, to abandon, to push a failing animal out into the winter cold.

Last week I met a woman in a broken-down hut. It was clearly not her home but she had somehow ended up there. She was very old. I could see she had not eaten in many days. She was thin and very ill. If she had been a man someone would have brought her something but she was just an old woman, some proud boy's mother, whose son was now gone and her husband long gone and her son's wife and grandchildren and servants all gone, and everyone pretended the hut was empty. Her shawl had once been brightly colored and fine. I tried to make her eat but she shooed me away from her. She shooed me out of the hut entirely, although she was almost too weak to move. She cursed me. She hurt me terribly and I cried very hard (just for a minute or two, in case a Japanese should see me) but then I thought her eyes had spoken to me, they had accepted some part of my food and my concern and had showed affection. Perhaps I'd reminded her of her eldest granddaughter. After that I felt relief and then I was angry. It was a painful and unnecessary experience; I wanted to send it away. I decided instead to make her my model, to behave as she did, except that I have no son and no family, no one to be reminded of by intruding strangers, and my eyes will be silent. I will become what she tried and failed to be. I hope she died, I wish her that. I hope she starved quickly and died.

I don't know why I am still intact; I don't know how I can have evaded harm for so long. I'm sure it has nothing to do with heaven. I have always felt that I mattered and was being watched over but at a time like this even heaven forgoes its concern for individuals to concentrate on history. And history now is that these murderers are destroying us and destroying our country. That is the essence of it. They are piling evil on evil. It is only simple luck that they have not destroyed me. Or perhaps not luck so much as something I am doing, perhaps lucky to be doing but also there may be some design to it, some useful pattern in my mind. I don't know what and I don't think I want to.

Understand: I have seen my sisters raped and lying by the road. I have seen the red limbs, twisted. But this has not come to me. I am ready for it—I think I have actually willed the nerves of my genitals to disappear, or to cease their function, and on some days I hardly know I have a sex at all—but it has not come. And I am equally ready for the bullet or the blade. I think I am a natural target but perhaps this is conceit, defying the endless suffering everywhere; the fact is that though there are many, many invaders there are many more of us, more even than they in their wild rage and lust can give attention to. And I have so far avoided all the wrong places, the ill-chosen times. In some fashion I have.

Perhaps I escape notice by being so dirty, so ragged, so stiff and so small. I am not aware of having worked at this, at least not for the purpose of saving myself, but I may have done it without my own knowledge; I am certainly very dirty and ragged, very stiff and repulsive, much more so than I would ever have guessed I could be. And I was always very plain. In any case they have not attacked me, they have not hurt me, they have not even spoken directly to me, and beyond that I have managed to find enough food to keep moving (though I am very thin) and for the most part have avoided the worst of the cold. In my own way I am blessed; I may be the only person in this part of China who is entirely without pain. I hesitate to say that I am still alive, that is hardly the word for it, but they have not killed me yet.

THREE

I am to stay here with the garrison. This morning I received the news from another captain, with whom I have slight and impersonal acquaintance. We passed in the muddy street in the center of town—I wandering to no purpose, trying to relieve both my boredom and the gloom that has been gathering around me with each passing day, he hurrying along with a fat folder under his arm—and he saluted and went a step or two farther before turning to walk alongside me. For some reason I refused to wait for him, but he kept pace.

"Had your orders?" he asked.

"No," I said, stopping then, "I've been away from camp."

He grinned. "We're on our way," he told me. "I'm so happy to get out of this place, even if we're going to another just like it." He was ready to say more but then his face changed.

"Tell me," I urged him.

"I'm sorry," he said. "I just remembered you're to stay here. I saw the papers. You're to command the garrison here. Yours was the listed name." I said nothing and he looked closely at me. I was cold standing there in the dirty street. His coat was better than mine. "Perhaps this is to your liking," he said.

"Either way," I replied. He continued to watch me. "I can serve either way," I went on, "or any other way the Emperor requires. All this petty speculation about decisions that don't concern us has annoyed me and I am glad we will be past it. I will be past it, at any rate, and good riddance." I admit to some pleasure at his confusion. As he tried to answer I looked around and saw clearly the large distances the Chinese were putting between us and themselves; there was a wide empty circle around us and as we were standing in the middle of the street this left the peasants to squeeze by in single file at the very edges, right up against the walls on either side. They were all dressed in rags and half-clothing of varying shades of brown. I doubt they knew our insignia but I am sure they could tell from our manner and attire that we were officers. As if this gave them greater reason to fear us! Even I fear the men more than I do my fellows, or myself, or the enemy.

"I'm eager to fight," he said, composure regained. "It's true we're not entitled to know before the proper time but after so much training and so many years it's very hard to sit and not fight." I nodded. "We all want to fight," he said.

"Of course," I said. "Please kill many for me. I won't have

the same opportunities here." Suddenly I wanted to shout it as loudly as I could, in the language of the vile pathetic creatures around me—PLEASE KILL AS MANY OF THESE AS YOU CAN FIND—and had I been able to I might have, were it not for the attention such behavior would have brought. (We officers are dignified and we seldom speak Chinese.) "Do your duty," I told him. I clapped him on the arm in a manly way and then gestured, a sort of partial bow attended by a tight fist of rage.

"And not just the Chinese, my friend," he said. "I expect to be fighting the whites before long. This is just a beginning, the opening event."

"Yes," I said. "The whites. I imagine they are better fighters."

"You could be right," he said. "Certainly they have better guns." He looked at his watch. "I'm late and I must go," he told me, bowing and saluting, then turning to rush down the street. The villagers parted before him so quickly I thought they would knock each other down. "Good luck," he called back to me.

"The Emperor," I replied.

Despite this news the day remained peculiarly static and pointless. On the way back to camp I found myself looking ceaselessly around me, as if expecting an attack. All I saw were the same shallow rolling hills and fields I have looked on every morning and evening for weeks. They are dark yellow and brown, and though they hold farms and houses they hold very little life. Behind me was the town I had just left, and here and there were huts and groups of huts and a few old and brittle-looking donkeys and goats. Pathetic rickety fences, what hadn't been torn down for firewood. Stands of stunted trees. The wind was blowing steadily but aside from the sound it made and the cry of an occasional bird—and the noise of two Japanese motorcycles that came past, each driver pretending not to see me and my captain's stars—it was very quiet. I might have been back in Manchuria. I might almost have been in a desert.

The winter has been much colder than we were given to expect and I am certain that in the summer the land is lush, but now it looks sterile and useless. Dry and unforgiving. They say it was all forest once, in ancient history. Then the hills were for trees and deer and wild boar, perhaps, and gentle streams; now they are for crops and livestock and Chinese shacks, all growing things it's true but they look barren to me. They don't look like places where humans can live. They seek cover from my eye.

As I walked I came across a scattered pile of cheaply printed papers, all red and white. I recognized them as propaganda flyers, dropped by our planes before the army arrived. Someone—some peasant—must have scavenged them for fuel and then lost them somehow (or perhaps he was set upon). I stooped to retrieve one and looked it over. Most of it was Chinese but the reverse said, in my language: "Any soldier bearing this paper and wishing to surrender must be accepted and protected as a voluntary prisoner." It was signed by the Commander in Chief of the Central China Expeditionary Force. I examined the front of the sheet again and noted several words: "friend," "prosperity," "instructions," "conspire." I thought back on some of the surrenders I had seen; I put the flyer in my pocket and went on, leaving the rest to blow across the road.

When I reached the main tent at headquarters Suzuki found me right away. He was furious. I had never before seen him genuinely indignant, only superior or officious or complaining but within it content. But now he was frantic and his lack of reserve, a hideous thing in any normal adult, was almost frightening. His voice rose from a hiss and threatened to become a shout. Even he in his rage saw the heads turn nearby and he took me outside.

"Where have you been?" he demanded.

"In the village," I said.

"What were you doing there?"

"Nothing," I told him. "Nothing specific or useful, Major. I was occupying time."

He actually stamped his foot, he was so angry. I could not understand why. I was a little worried that he would assault me; I knew he wanted to, and felt that if I said the wrong thing he might.

"Suzuki-dono, I am sorry," I said.

"Keep your mouth shut," he said. "How did you get there?"

"I walked."

"And back?"

"I walked."

He glared at me. "I have several things for you to know," he said. "First, the general and his staff have been waiting for you. Yes! Waiting! For you! You were instructed to be available. You had no orders to go to town. In any case you had no business exposing yourself to risk by walking. That was an explicit violation of orders! You wasted an entire morning and kept a general waiting and the shame you would have brought on me had you been attacked and killed on the road is maddening to consider. What can possibly have made you behave in this way?"

Then I understood his emotion. To keep a general waiting must have been torture to him. He had been fearing for his future and also (I had to be fair to him) for mine. Despite his hints and implications it was probably rare for him to meet with a general—presumably from what he said there really was a general somewhere nearby—and for a general to directly order him to do anything, and in this instance he had failed. Thanks to me. With such a turn of events he had risen entirely out of his depth and I felt sorry for him. He would probably be frantic for the rest of the war.

"Stupidity, Major," I answered. "Stupidity and lack of personal discipline. Inability to be orderly and patient. I *am* shamed." I could not look at him; I stared at the mud and a tent peg. "I will apologize to the general."

"You will not!" he hissed. "Do not pretend to me. That is intolerable. I will not have it! We are not two intellectuals chatting now over tea, we are soldiers in the Imperial Army and *they will shoot us*. Do you comprehend it? They will shoot us if it suits them."

"Surely not for being absent when the general calls."

I looked up to see his lips tight, his eyes filled with power. "Kuroda, you ignorant fool," he said. "You idiot. I had thought you were learning. I had thought you wiser. Look around you. Does this look like your university?" His voice was almost choking. "They will discard you unless you are useful," he told me. "They will discard you! Do you understand?"

I looked away. I thought of my wife.

"Do you understand?" he asked.

"I do," I said.

We stood waiting together.

"There was a reason for your absence," he said. "A fight among the troops, perhaps, or a theft of food by locals. I will explain, and *I* will do the apologizing." I heard him sigh—I was still looking away, standing almost rigid though I had not realized it until just then—and he put his hand on my shoulder. "We are to be separated, you know," he said. "They have a job for you."

"I heard," I said. "I was told. By an officer in town. Who laughed at me for it."

"Responsibility," he assured me. "A difficult task."

GET YOUR HAND OFF MY SHOULDER, I wanted to tell him. I wanted to strike him down. YOU ARE DIRT TO ME. But reduced as I am to the mandatory truthfulness that follows me everywhere I also knew that Suzuki, for all his sloppy anxiety, his exaggerated self-expression, reminded me very much of my father. There is no man less like my father but I felt myself to be at that moment a small boy, and Suzuki a strong man. As if I had just lost my kite to the wind.

"I'll be alone," I told him.

"I'll be back," he said. "Don't worry, my duties will bring me back to you. Make no mistake.

FOUR

Today I washed my clothing. I could almost believe that everything was as it had been. There were about a dozen of us there—mostly women but also two men, who'd been reduced to it—and we were all strong enough to walk to the river and scrub, all physically intact (as far as I could see) and not starved to death yet. Besides, there is something about washing clothing that denies the existence of the very last extremity; the fact that we were there at all, on that errand, implied that we had hope. The clothes themselves were terrible in every case, there wasn't a piece that wouldn't have been discarded by any but the beggars before the war came, but at least the motions were familiar, and we might have been washing fine garments instead. Though I knew none of the others and in fact exchanged no words with them and not even a friendly glance (unless you count the appraising look of the younger man, who considered me for a replacement wife), I felt almost kindly. It seemed they were my family. Despite myself I was temporarily transformed, or at least my view of the world and my place in it was, and for half an hour I forgot that I was miles from my home and lost in Wan Dong; I felt entitled again, only slightly but very definitely, as surely as if I'd had coins in my pocket. I tried to resist this—distant and frightened is the way I wish to be—but I couldn't. A separate fraction of me entirely, insensible to discipline and mortification, wanted to lie down in the sun.

A notable thing about that stretch of the river is that the banks are high for quite a distance, but with broad flat areas at the bottom, which I imagine the water covers for a few weeks in the spring. If I stood in the right spot it was almost as if I was in a tiny valley; I couldn't see anything more than thirty feet from the water on either side, because the bank cut off my view. We were evenly spread out over three or four hundred feet—for modesty's sake and to avoid fouling each other's laundry—and all that space and order also worked to undermine me. It gave me a sense of ease, almost of luxury. All was quiet, for the moment, at least in our false river valley. Once when the sun went behind a cloud I shivered, and wished the riverbanks really were mountains ten thousand feet high, with the soldiers and hunger and blood on the other side, but as the light returned my universe contracted and limited itself again to an earthen depression with water flowing through it. I was content not to recognize anything further. At the far end of the line the older man had built a fire to dry us out—I had put my things on wet despite the chill, if I was proud enough to wash my clothes I wasn't going to stand around naked—and as I walked toward it I felt myself to be a dancer in a stage play, or a monk in a ritual; I felt I was following instructions and doing rather well at that. A sort of happy surrender came over me, a stupid release, and while a part of me asked whether the smoke was a dangerous thing the rest was foolishly hoping that when I reached it one of the women would take me in her arms (I was far the youngest one) and dote on me as a child, and let me drowse by the flame.

Of course this did not happen but while I stood there, drying myself and staring at the sand, I maintained within my mind this lack of alarm. It wasn't that everything was going to be all right—I continued to understand, for instance, that I would be dead within a month—but that everything was all right at that time and place, the danger present but not then threatening. Which was enough for me. I looked at the ground, partly out of shame for my immodest appearance and partly to avoid the others' eyes, but mostly to curtail my perspective even further. I wanted everything drawn in to that one gentle, peaceful spot. To the wet fabric on my body, which smelled good (or had stopped smelling bad) for the first time in days. To my not-so-empty belly (I'd begged rice from a farmer) and my rested limbs (I'd slept comfortably in the hog pen, the hogs stolen long since). I almost fell asleep and started dreaming like that, or perhaps I entered a trance; given the choice, I know, I would have kept it thus forever. I would be standing there at this moment and even a thousand years from now.

Feeling warm in my breasts and thighs at last I turned the other side of me to the fire, and as I did I looked up. On the bank to the east stood a Japanese officer. He was looking right at me, right at my face. I wanted to be frightened—I felt I should be—but I stayed calm. Though he was forty yards away he looked straight into my eyes. His bearing told me that he was not important. He was not tall, not strong. His uniform was worn but somehow stiff; his hands rested at his waist. We looked at each other for a very long time—there is no way I could put a precise duration on it but it was more than a moment, more than four moments, or ten—and I remained content. That is, I did not want to be elsewhere. I did not want him to stop looking at me. I did not even want him to draw his gun and kill me. He was waiting for some reason and I was as patient as he.

From my left I heard a sound, a single spoken word, and though I didn't turn my head I saw his eyes shift to one side and the other and I knew they had seen him. I knew they too were frozen in place. Though small he was a giant standing up there, the afternoon sun lighting him. He was a statue, a memorial, a man of basalt. His eyes moved slowly among us as he waited.

Suddenly he shouted and gestured. He was pointing at the top of the bank beside him; it was clear that he wanted us to climb it. His expression was hard, though not angry. This was the end, I knew: they would shoot us now. Because we'd started a fire or polluted the water upstream of the troops or just because we were there and so were they, and we were not them and they were not us. Perhaps they would toy with us in some way but probably not. They would just bayonet us. We weren't worth the cost of bullets. They would leave us to bleed into the ground.

I was the first to reach the top, where he was, and while the others were still climbing he barked in Japanese again and pointed across the river to the west. This time I understood him, though his accent was strange; what he said was "They are leaving us." I kept my eyes on his face because I was afraid to follow his gesture, afraid to see my fate, but he shouted "Look!" and pointed again, urgently, his left hand on his sword. I turned—preferring a rifle or even the trooper's filthy steel to being personally murdered by this small impatient man—and there in the distance, on the road, was his army. It looked like every one of them, like every beast soldier in China. The sun came down behind them. The road made its way around and over the low hills, switching back and forth, and there was an enormous column of soldiers marching on it, from horizon to horizon, filling it completely, and there were trucks and guns and horses. They were going north and a little bit west, away from where we were and away from the village to the south. I had never seen anything so powerful in my life. It was a huge crawling black snake which could have entered me at one end and left at the other and exploded me to pieces without even noticing what it had done. It was God leaving a trail across the earth. I caught my breath and filled my lungs because I was sure they were taking the air with them, taking all the food, taking even the light—the sun was going with them and guarding their passage—and I wanted to save just a little for myself.

I could see, without looking, the others standing nearby, as still and silent as I. (I could hear the small sounds of their breathing and their feet shifting on the soil, but that was all.) The wind was steady and it froze me as it dried my clothes while I stood and watched. It could not have been very long but it seems to me—remembering it—that the day became more yellow, more golden, even as we stood there, that it changed and promised night.

"They are going," he said. "They are leaving me." I glanced at him and then all around us, to discover that he was alone. There were no soldiers with him; the only gun present was his pistol, the only blade his sword. Still, it would have been easy for him to kill us. There was no one there to witness it; just our odd group on the river bank and the nearby fields and a few sorry animals and scattered huts and workers and then the town and then the hills, with a black snake strangling them. He could have shot the two men and me and the one other woman who looked at all vigorous and then cut the rest to bits. But he didn't seem interested in that. Instead he peered from face to face to make sure we had all seen the marching troops. "You're too stupid and terrified to make anything of it," he said. "You're not even glad to see them go." It was clear that he did not expect to be understood, so I tried very hard to hide my understanding; I thought he would kill me if he knew.

Suddenly he rushed up to the older of the two men, an obvious tenant farmer who was probably under fifty but looked ancient due to work and deprivation. "Down!" he shouted, and slapped the man's face viciously. The peasant just stood there and the Japanese slapped him again and shouted "Down!" and stamped, and then in his insistent fury—there was no way for the man to have known what was wanted, he didn't speak Japanese and the officer had not even gestured, merely shouted—he grabbed him by the collar and pushed him to his knees. The peasant fell easily, pliantly, as he probably had many times before, and waited for whatever was coming with no sign of fear or resistance, or even sadness. I was reminded of my own state before the officer arrived (peace is acquiescence; acquiescence is peace), and as I prepared to watch him killed I considered that perhaps this was their purpose in coming to our country and doing all their evil: to reduce us to that condition. To gut us. To destroy our desire and our urgency. To make us chronically content as long as the metal is not, at that instant, tearing through our bowels or smashing into our brains.

The Japanese walked a step or two away from the older man, then returned to him. He slapped him across the cheek once more, but with far less force, almost gently. "You're worthless," he said to all of us, quietly. "You benefit no one. If I could I'd send you off to die with them." His expression was both bitter and hurt; he was, I realized, at least as far from home as I. He looked at me again, looked directly into my eyes, and I despaired of convincing him that I didn't understand. The long dark worm moved on the hills behind him and he looked at me and asked a question. "When will this end?" he asked me. "When will it end?" He stared at me for a moment more and turned away. Then he approached the kneeling peasant, pulling him to his feet, and walked off toward the town, his hands clasped behind his back. His step was brisk.

The other women were still stiff with fear. Two of them began to talk quietly, murmuring, their eyes on the officer as they watched him go. Mine were on the hills. Then I saw the younger man approach the elder and examine his face. I looked also and while there were bruises forming it would be no worse than that.

"They're not so bad," said the young man. He laughed,

briefly—an amazing thing—and started down the bank towards the fire.

"They're raping murdering scum," I told him. "You've seen the corpses."

He stopped and turned to me. There was a foul and confident cast to his eye that I hadn't noticed before.

"I saw corpses before they ever came," he said. "I've seen them all my life. There are always corpses and they always stink."

I said nothing. In the distance were the burdened hills.

He started down again, then stopped once more and faced me. He almost smiled. "They could have taken care of you," he said, looking me up and down. "You know they could have but they didn't. They could have done you very well."

If I close my eyes I picture it; when I sleep I sometimes dream of it, though this is fortunately rare. I will always stand in that city, watching, with my hands at my sides. I will always see it. It fills me with grief to think that I might by chance have been elsewhere, and so missed it, and thus escaped the curse of knowing.

I am saturated with disgust. I am drenched in loathing and dismay, but here I am. It would not end; there was no end; for weeks it went on without pause, without respite for anyone—Chinese, Japanese, Europeans, me—and when at last it began to subside it did so not because it was finished but because there was a surfeit: too many screams, too many ashes, too much blood. The system was clogged, choked with torn-up human refuse, and the living were exhausted, and the men reluctantly agreed among themselves that it was time for them to stop. You could see it in their eyes—I DO NOT WANT TO BUT I MUST—and in the way their sadism diminished in scale, but not in kind, as if a knob had been turned: random murder and mutilation replaced by careful kicks to the spine and the groin, heedless rape made methodical and selective, almost conservative (out of necessity, perhaps, to save some for future pleasure), the children finally left alone except for the threat of their destruction as a means of coercing their parents into whatever was desired. Ultimately there was a shortage of victims, as well as a limit to the army's capacity. Someone had to be left to carry the water, to clear the streets.

In this country I have learned about images, about visions, both real and imagined. I understand now what makes the painter work his paper (at least more than I once did). What is seen can be recorded; what is recognized is seen. I am reminded of my textbooks and their diagrams of leaves. I cannot become less familiar with Suzuki's face than I am at this moment, if I never meet him again, nor can I forget the structure of *Palmaria palmata*. I cannot become a stranger to my mother's blackened rice pot. I can never leave Nanking.

My fellow officers and I were at the center of it. Our cowardice, unavoidable, settled on and covered us as a terrible miasma—a stink like that which rose from our surroundings every hour of every day—as if our own limbs were rotting on our bodies. To say that we lost control of our men would be a falsehood; it was much worse than that. It was much worse. To say, even, that they forgot our existence would be wrong. In fact they invited us to join them—they demanded that we join them—and most did. (My own saber was taken from me one day, pulled from its very scabbard, by a colonel who needed it at just that moment; I avoided knowledge of his actions only by closing my eyes, then turning my back, then walking around the corner, and even so I can guess what he used it for.) Those weeks did little more than describe us, really, as what we honestly were, fulfilling our fates and condemning us in the process. It shocked me very deeply but it ventured nothing new. As the work of our hands gave way to machines, as the last century turned to this, as Korea led to Manchuria and Manchuria to the bridge and the bridge to Peking and Peking to Shanghai and Shanghai to that foul, cursed, exploded city, bathed in pain and seething with a brutal joyless glee, so our presence there and our very natures led to the crimes we committed; so the Chinese and Japanese essences mingled and battled and congealed into what might once have been monstrous inconceivable error but became, easily, naturally, as dawn turns to day, the new face of the world. I am lucky to have been there. I am lucky that I know. I can count myself one of the almost prepared.

Perhaps someday, if I survive this war and everything that must follow, someday decades from now, I will silently sit for an hour or two over tea with a stranger, and then begin to disemburden myself to ears that will never hear me again, to he who will never know my name. Perhaps if I cover my eyes as I speak. I can hear myself reciting, unimpassioned, sitting comfortably in my chair—starting from the beginning and moving chronologically or by category, whichever is preferred—recalling the incidents one by one. I have an eye for detail and so my listener will not be deprived of the essence of it, the most important facts: the purple color of the silk of a merchant's wife's pants leg, as she is thrown to the earth; the high-pitched hysterical wailing sound made by small Chinese children; the smell of burning flesh; the words that can be heard among the cheers of the soldiers watching a tenement collapse on its occupants, in a shower of embers and brick and tile; the finely carved figures on the ancient stone monument against which rest various disconnected portions of human anatomy, like rifles stacked by a wall between battles. It will take an evening, a night, or maybe more for me to tell it. What I gathered to myself under conditions I had never remotely imagined will be returned, I am certain, in its own fashion, in whatever way it requires, probably one phrase at a time and slowly too. It will have a path to follow. It will insist. As a vessel of history I am not ideal, I admit; my only qualifications are that attachment to detail, lifelong, and the fact that I was there.

I don't expect to be believed. It will be much easier—and more logical, more sane—to assume hallucination, or even lies. The past will rise up and swallow all. Surely the others will never tell what they did; surely those who did nothing will never tell what they witnessed. I was there and I may tell but I expect to be alone.

What did I see? I saw rape, constant rape: Japanese soldiers copulating with countless Chinese women in the open air on the frozen ground, white breath-vapor rising, crying infants nearby, and stabbing them when finished. I saw stacks and stacks of bodies. I saw schoolchildren chased through the streets by laughing men who killed them when they caught them, or let them live with pieces gone. I saw prisoners marched into pits and covered over. I saw prisoners set afire. I saw a bayonet enter the abdomen of a naked pregnant woman and though I prayed not to catch sight of the child and was spared this, I cannot forget that I watched the blade open up the outer skin, and then penetrate the womb. Perhaps the image I remember is my own diseased invention—what is recognized is seen—but I know that this happened. I know my own ears heard the sound.

In full embrace I hold these things; I know them as well as I know my father's fingers. We ache together. I am loyal to them, and they to me.

One might hope as a consequence of living thus through hell for the diminution of vision, the curtailment of experience, the gradual withdrawal of one's natural talents. One might hope that the inability to ever see anything uncorrupted again might be countered, at least in time, by the inability to see at all. So far I have no sign of this; if anything my sight is sharpened. Therefore my stranger will not have finished with me, when I finish with that place. There will be an after to be told about, always an after. The record of these following days.

That was chaos but this is calm. That was a roaring, a clashing, a full-throated desperate continuous cry; here there are whispers and frequently silence. I came out of that wilderness into this and either way I am lost, directionless, no chance to find the East and turn my face toward home, not even as an exercise to strengthen my heart. I know what I have seen here, and it sticks to me, but I can't look on what I long for. I want not to open my eyes.

But I am forced to. I am forced to. And then what do I see? I see my own bloodied hands; I see the careful faces of my men, who were there, who took those actions, who eat their rations, who carry photographs of their friends and of their families and of kimonoed movie stars neatly tucked inside their tunics; I see the city in its silence only fifty miles away. I see Chinese heads, Chinese feet, Chinese backs, and a billion more behind them. I see my own look of contempt. I see my wife in our home, cooking rice, and our daughter at her school, and imperial servants hurrying back and forth over palace terraces, in the fading winter sun.

What else do I see? I see a nation defended. I see a giant tidal wave. I see a rotting small Japan, a Japan of the weak and the frightened, living in damp caves, speaking ever more softly, serving out the sentence of its shame forever.

There is a circle of betrayal here, a perfect closed phenomenon like the movement of sap within a tree, or the cycle of the seasons. We each have our valued role. I betrayed my men and they betrayed their families and we all betrayed the Emperor; and the Emperor betrayed me. I don't know why he would do it. I don't know why. I don't claim to understand. If I still believed in heaven I might imagine it differently, but I don't and so I can't. On some days now I am not even Japanese.

Despise me as a traitor—it's the only thing to do. As I rest here in this dirty, windy, useless foreign land.

The man who captured me is not a soldier. I am certain of that. He is Japanese and wears a uniform and officer's markings but he was not bred to this army, nor welcomed to it, and he intends to leave it when he has the opportunity. When his emperor allows him to, I suppose; when the war is over and we are all dead and broken and they have made wide bridges across the Huang Hai to Korea and Japan.

He doesn't like to be here and would leave us undisturbed but this is not out of kindness or pity. He has no thought for us. What he has seen here puzzles him; he rejects it; he wishes it away, and when he opens his eyes it is still all around him. *We* are all around him. It isn't difficult to know him: I see him on the floor of a paper room on

Hokkaido, studying a book, a cup of tea at hand, nervous and annoyed when a truck passes on the road outside his house. I see a family, a small garden. I see him talking briskly to the manager of his bank, a bank with headquarters in Tokyo and offices everywhere, even Singapore, and if that bank has not the resources another will provide. All this I can see clearly in his face as I watch him, as he stares hopelessly out over his new and worthless territory. But I do not see a fighter. I do not see a soldier. I do not see a man who should by any means be here. He knows nothing of the country; if not for his restlessness, his strong sense of displacement, I think he might actually be bored. We have made no impression on him, none at all. In his case they chose most poorly.

This is the man who found us with our laundry at the river that day, who struck the peasant and spoke to me. It has been over a week since then and I was very frightened at the river and I have seen and avoided several different Japanese, but I am sure this is the one. I can't remember his face—because I thought he would kill me I refused to inform myself of it, though I looked into his eyes—but the voice is very familiar, the stance, the way of moving. Even his graying head. It isn't a surprise; I saw the army leave that afternoon without him and I suppose I have been waiting for him since. I knew he was still here, that it was just a question of time. Even if he were another small, drab, unhappy Japanese officer it wouldn't make any difference, they are in my eye interchangeable, but he is certainly the same. I remember him.

This time I was glad to see him. I thought my luck had run out at last and I was preparing myself to be taken. A group of drunken soldiers had somehow found me in that night's sleeping place—a nest of straw and dirt under the porch of a cottage near the edge of the village—and had pulled me out to look me over. I could smell the rice wine in their mouths. It was very early in the morning, in the dim light a few minutes before the sun comes up, and I had been lying awake, deciding to go south. I had been telling myself for weeks that I could make it through the winter but that morning, just before they found me, I had allowed myself to understand that I was cold in a way I had never been before, probably from thinness and hunger, and that I could not remove this sensation from my body as I had most of the feeling from my soul, that it was wearing and upsetting me. There were just six weeks, at most, until warmer weather came—assuming that the war had not actually harmed the earth enough to unbalance the seasons—but that was too much, I acknowledged. I would fall ill in that time and become easy prey. I was gathering myself to crawl out and stand and move quietly away when I heard their voices and the sounds of their boots, and though I kept myself still one of them came directly to me, as if he could smell me, and reached in to take hold of me, and pulled me out in one rough motion like a man immensely strong. Another of them laughed and tossed his cigarette away.

I lay there on the ground with dirt on my face. There were four of them. They were as surprised as I was, I think, and for a moment they didn't know what to do with me. What they probably wanted most was their beds. I found it odd—incredible that with all the effort I've made it was still possible for me to retain my judgment, my curiosity even, at such a moment—that they would be allowed to drink and stay out all night. I heard a faint sound from inside the cottage and I knew its occupants were awake and terrified. I wondered if they understood what was happening and I hoped that they didn't, to spare them more distress; they could do nothing for me. There was a brief exchange between the soldiers, too fast and slurred for me to follow, and one began to walk away. A second turned to go after him but a third—the light was a little stronger but it was very hard for me to make his every motion out—dropped his gun to the ground and began to unfasten his pants.

The last one stepped back and aimed his weapon at me. I guessed that he wanted me to resist, so he could shoot me, and I weighed this course of action, but it soon occurred to me that he did not want to kill me; he wanted to maim me and watch his companion rape me anyway. Better, I thought, if you're going to do anything other than lie here limp, to try to hurt him once he's in you. Then the other will kill you to protect him. The thought of dying with the man inside me was intriguing, almost humorous as I lay there, watching him remove his tunic. Would he go ahead and finish? He looked reluctant and moved slowly, as if performing a chore—perhaps the unwilling accomplice of his partner, who took no pleasure from fucking a Chinese woman but enjoyed shooting her before she was fucked, while she was fucked, after she was fucked by somebody else—and I considered speaking to him in his own language. But I didn't know what to say, and whatever I said would almost certainly make it worse. I wanted to be raped only once, or at most twice, and to die quickly. That was what I bargained for, what my outlook had diminished to.

Then I heard a nearly familiar voice. "Stop it," it said in Japanese. "What are you doing?" The soldiers were instantly upright, one looking ludicrous in his undershirt in the frigid air, with his belt-ends dangling, the other grounding his rifle. I heard regular steps, unhurried, the sound of boots making their way through the yard. At first I didn't want to see him, I didn't want to move, but I risked a glance. I saw the officer coming toward me. The sun had started rising on the other side of the cottage and for a moment he was orange-lit before he came into the shadow of the building, where we were. I turned my face skyward again and closed my eyes and waited.

"Well?" he asked. "What are you doing?" There was silence. "Were you about to attack this woman? Why?" I couldn't imagine them having an answer—it was such a stupid question—and they didn't. I wondered if he was making some amusement of his own and would simply leave in the end and let them finish what they'd started. I wondered if he was crazy. I began to hate him fiercely for prolonging my suffering; I wanted to feel the hard flesh and the steel and have it over with.

"Put your clothes on," he said. I couldn't see him but I could see the others, and as I watched the soldier quickly closed his pants and pulled on his tunic. "You'll get pneumonia and die and I can't spare you," the officer said. "Don't think I don't know you've been drinking as well. You're a bad joke and I would shoot you myself but as I said I can't spare you. Get back to the barracks this instant." The first soldier stooped to get his gun and then they both saluted and began to back away from us.

In that moment I asked myself, what was this man doing here? How did he come to be wandering the village at such an hour? Why would he bother to interfere?

"Stop," called the officer. The soldiers, who had turned their backs, turned around again, rigidly at attention. "If I ever find you doing this to another woman I *will* shoot you. You're an embarrassment to the homeland." They continued to stand there, watching him. "Get out of here," he said.

He walked to a spot by my feet so he could look down at my face. "Unremarkable," he said.

"Thank you," I said.

He started. "Did you say 'thank you'?" he asked.

"Yes," I said. "Thank you for stopping them."

He frowned. "I didn't do it for you," he said. "They're pigs. Worthless." I said nothing but I heard the sound of my breath, passing through my nostrils. It had become very loud.

"How is it that you speak Japanese?" he asked.

"My father taught me."

"Your accent is bad."

"That doesn't surprise me. I don't know many words either."

He stood there and looked down on me. His hands were on his hips. He was very composed and his uniform was stiff and carefully arranged; it was almost impossible to believe that he would appear as he did at such a time, in such a place. It was comic. He was a picture. He didn't move, didn't speak, and I felt he was content to look down on me forever.

"How did your father learn Japanese?" he asked at last.

I was too exhausted to lie. "He studied medicine in Japan," I said. I hesitated. "His mother was Japanese."

The officer coughed as he looked at me. I became, to my amazement, a little angry.

"Do you mind if I stand?" I asked. "It's very cold down here."

I was further amazed when he stepped forward and held out his hand. I sat up and took it—he wore gloves and there was no warmth in his fingers—and raised myself to my feet. He was small but had the strength to hold me firmly as I rose. As I brushed myself off he continued to stare at me—I had the definite sense that he was seeing me very clearly, very particularly, but also looking at some other thing separate from me, something with which I had no common thread—and I thought he was fascinated by what I'd told him. I was sure that he was. I regretted the revelation; I'd tried so hard for so long to conceal my strange connection to them and now it had come out. I wondered what he would do about it. But I was utterly astonished when he shook his head, coughed again, looked at me once more, then turned and walked away.

I said: "They'll come back for me eventually, you know."

He stopped and faced me. We were several yards apart.

"What are you doing sleeping in barnyards?" he asked me. "That is no way for an educated person to live."

"I have no choice," I said. "My home was ruined."

"Nearby?"

"No. In Kiangsu."

"Why don't you go to the city?" he asked, almost clinically, as if detached from my circumstance. As if he'd had nothing to do with it. "There is civil authority there."

"I'm an unprotected woman."

"You are intelligent. You speak Japanese. Surely someone would assist you."

I was hard put not to laugh. I believe he saw this in me. It was getting lighter all the time and we could both see more than we had. We watched each other and it seemed he was making calculations, guardedly, somewhere within.

"What is your name?" he asked.

"Li."

"Is that your family name?"

"What does it matter?"

I hadn't meant to speak that way and I didn't think he would tolerate it, but he just stood a little straighter and sighed, deeply, staring at me—his hands behind his back now—and slowly nodded.

"Can you cook?" he asked. "And clean?"

I too nodded slowly.

"I suppose you'd better come with me," he said.

SEVEN

The woman I'm protecting is no ordinary Chinese. I sensed this the first time I saw her. Not on the ground outside that pitiful hovel at dawn; I remember now that I saw her before. She was one of the women washing rags in the river. Rags—and only that. And less a river than a stream. I remember her there, I think I spoke to her. Of course I am now aware that she understood my words—imagine finding in this desolate place a woman, a woman! who speaks Japanese, wandering filthy and gaunt from one dirthole to the next—but as I recall I said nothing then that shamed me. I was upset, bitter. I took the opportunity to utter to uncomprehending Chinese what I could not to my men, and very little of that. Still, the circumstance was awkward; it was wise of her to stay quiet. I was far from myself. I might even have harmed her.

There was something that distinguished her that day by the water, not only from those near her but from all the others, all the people I have seen here. What was it? I want to say a special quality, a gentleness or nobility, but I don't know what that means; when I think of such things I am no longer certain of whether my toughts are my own or instead an artifact of propaganda, a distorted reflection of our other-hating rage. Must I now begin to grade people like fishes? In Japan I knew who I was: a Japanese man who thought more of the outside world and less of Japan than most of my associates. Educated, enlightened, probably effete, possibly un-Japanese, but I kept it to myself. Even my wife, with her distaste for the blind nationalists, the warmongers, was secure in her assessment of the peoples of the earth: hers came first. First by right. And in essence I agreed with her, though I qualified it. It was a comfortable way to be; I knew my sort was better than the rest and I knew I was better than the rest of my sort, because I recognized the limits of our superiority and held some interest in, some sympathy for those to whom we were superior. It was simple and I never had reason to question it.

But in China it is difficult. I see each day how much better we really are in some ways and it gives me ever greater reason to wonder what this should imply. We are superior to them but we are not ourselves worth praising. And by our actions here alone they are far better than we, we are the worst. We are the basest. I am the tool of my country: I am required to discard these people, to believe they are not human, and I do it because I must. But it spreads itself to me and to my soldiers, to all the other Japanese, it taints us all. ALL RIGHT, I say often, WE ARE NONE OF US HUMAN. WE ARE ALL THE SAME DUST.

So perhaps this is why I saw something in Li (is that really her name?). Perhaps this is why I see it in her. To remind me of myself. Because I now accept their lies. Because I need to believe that if she is special the others are common, and their loss is no great loss, their pain no grievous pain. I have no confidence at all. Does it help to understand that she is partly Japanese? Does it clarify the picture? No, it makes it more difficult, more clouded; it tightens up my chest. Is it useful to know that her father was a doctor, that he traveled to Japan? Imagine the other students laughing at him, taunting him, spitting on him! Imagine starting at a given position, a sensible place, and being guided along a certain path, and ending up somewhere with that sense turned upside down. That is what happened to him; that is what has happened to me. I cannot be expected to see my situation clearly. They have robbed me of my past and I am mortally confused. What do I think of her? And she of me? I have no confidence at all.

She sleeps in the outer room, next to the stove. She makes meals and launders my clothing and sweeps. When I speak to her she answers. She sits and stares out at the hills.

When I look at her I see: a plain young Chinese woman, taller than most but not too tall, dressed in the clean, rough simple clothing found for her by one of my soldiers. Her skin is good on the whole. There is a small but peculiar scar on the rear portion of her right cheek, near the back point of the jaw. She walks with independence, even pride, but at the same time she has manners and great dignity. Her joints are loose. Her wrists are small. I know she was raised by loving parents. I know she was never hungry before this year.

Her accent and vocabulary are rapidly improving, though we don't really converse.

I do not want her here. I have no interest in her. I have no interest in any Chinese, I have no interest in this country, I have no interest in my life until they give it back to me and allow me to go home but I am also a man and she is young, healthy, in no way crippled or disfigured. She is at my absolute command and depends on me for life. It makes me anxious. I can barely stand her near me. So far I am behaving well but for how long? How long? It is convenient to have a servant but anything I need done I can do for myself or make the soldiers do. It would be better not to have her here. I question my motives. And how on earth can she trust me, even slightly? After everything that's happened?

In the end I may try to arrange for her passage to the southwest, away from us. I will try my best to do it. Of course I cannot assist her in actually crossing the lines but she seems resourceful; after she has gained a little weight (I made it clear to her that she should take what she needs from the meals she prepares for me) and recovered some of her strength, she should be able to slip through.

I hear her speak again and again: "They'll come and get me soon enough."

Why did I not let them go ahead? What was she to me? There are no brothels here, there are not enough of us for it to be worth the army's while. And of course soldiers will rape. I had that proved to me before. What a painful joke for me to think—after everything I saw!—that it matters one grain of rice, one fly, whether a certain Chinese woman is violated and killed or maimed. There are millions of them. Many millions. Why did I take a stand, brand myself eccentric, undermine my own authority to protect one young woman who will, as she said, be taken sooner or later in any event? We will be here for years at the least, perhaps decades. She may grow old among the soldiers. I might have let her get on with it, with her suffering, might have even let her out of it if I had allowed them to finish her off. She might have been free. Now she is getting used to warmth and food and sleep and cleanliness again, even kind words (I try not to but I can't help myself at times) and recovering a sense of security, possibly even hope, and to what purpose? To what purpose? So she can be raped later, in a month or a year? Be exploded by a bomb? Contract typhus? Be shot? Perish delivering a half-Japanese baby? Starve to death? Beg away the rest of her days on the ruined streets of Soochow or Shanghai?

This horrid arrogance they've taught me. This hollow strutting pose.

Well, I stopped them—it was insane but I did it—and now here we are. Sharing two rooms in a commandeered school. Waiting for nothing to happen, for Suzuki to come back, for my soldiers to do more damage to this country so I can discipline them for it. For the enemy to fight us. Waiting for the soil of Asia to rise up and throw me back to Japan. For the waters of the East China Sea to rush inland and wipe us all away.

Just as I hear her voice on that morning I also see her face. Watching me. From the ground, watching me. I see it. I wanted to go; I tried to get away. It was her idea, not mine.

When she told me "thank you" of course I had to answer. I had to answer something. And as I did so it hit me that she had spoken Japanese. Could I let that pass? Could I? She was a person; she was in distress. After hearing the odd details of her pitiful story I tried to cut it short, I tried to spare us both any more humiliation. She chose not to let me so I undertook to advise her. To suggest the city was stupid but it was what I had to say; I am not responsible for them all. At least I offered her something. And she had the courage or the foolishness to speak with disrespect to me, to talk back, and I had to press my point for honor's sake. My own effete, enlightened kind of honor; else I would have shot her. I was the Emperor's officer!—she a filthy conquered subject. And I tried to reason with her.

"You speak Japanese," I said. "Surely someone would protect you."

She looked at me with such contempt that I wanted to strike her face.

And then she stood there waiting for me, waiting for something, I don't know what, not for me to speak or act on behalf of Japan and all the harm we've done, the things we've robbed her of, not to hurt or kill her or take care of her or provide for her but something else, some sort of communication, some statement or attachment or display. She looked right into me, with eyes like the earth; she touched my very bottom. I was fixed to the spot.

"I can cook," she said. "And I can clean." And then she waited.

So I gestured her to follow.

MOUNTAIN

EIGHT

His chambers are ugly. At least it is warm here. The soldiers fill the stove up twice a day, with captured coal—there can't be any fuel in the entire Middle Kingdom that hasn't been appropriated by the Japanese, other than sticks and paper and straw—and all the windows are well sealed. The warmth restores my body to me. I had almost forgotten what it was like to use my nose, for example; when I was out in the cold it was a breather rather than a smeller, an opening for air instead of a portal of the senses, and only now does its former function return.

There is much to smell in these rooms. It keeps my nostrils very busy. I cook several different foods here and I clean with lots of soap, and there are also the smells left over from before the war, the smells from twenty years of use. And I can smell myself again.

I also smell him. I can't help it; we sleep just thirty feet apart. Especially when I pass by the closed door of his bedroom I smell him, even more than when I enter there to clean. His odor leaks out around the edges, into the larger chamber. It is the contrast that I smell.

This was once the district school, a very unappealing building. It is modern and well made but even so I can't admire it. They have made it much worse, of course, by taking down everything of any possible aesthetic value: every poster, every decoration, even the blackboards. (I observe this as an indication of who these people are. I might have guessed he would have left at least one picture hanging but he apparently chose not to.) Here and there on the walls are grayish military documents and notices, but that is all. Our rooms were the teacher's quarters, almost certainly, though there are now bullet holes outside the door. It was an extremely un-Chinese building to begin with—who knows why they built it in this humble, hidden place—and I hate to picture the children coming to it every morning, leaving China and crossing the border into their little bit of somewhere else. It makes me very sad. But this is worse; it's even sadder to think that what was once the only agent of progress in their lives, the only attention to their futures, now belongs to the emperor of Japan. It is occupied and annexed and I am its only native, its silent spy. No wonder that I loathe it. It is my punishment to be here.

His smell is alien; I don't know about a Japanese smell but his is foreign, peculiar, distant, odd. It makes me think of Canton when I traveled there with my mother as a girl, not because it is like Canton but because my eyes were so wide open and I paid such close attention and I *remembered* Canton, remembered clearly every bit of it. Because it was so very far away. After that Canton was always *different* to me, it was the place that Wasn't Home, and no matter how bored and dull I became from the sameness of life and unchanging days I could think back on it and summon the strange sights and sounds, the intriguing aromas, and regain that sense that somewhere else was in the world. Somewhere not the same. His odor is like that—an exotic experience—but with fear added in. With worry and anger. As if I'd been born fifty years earlier, been taken south at twelve to be married off and left there, not to play the pampered darling of my father's wealthy cousins.

He asked me once about Canton; he asked me if I'd been. I said I hadn't. He said he'd read of it as a child.

My routine is fairly simple here. I wake up very early. I open the stove and rake the coals together to get a hot spot, and make him tea and rice for breakfast. I have a little tea myself. (Ten weeks without tea! I can hardly believe it. I don't know how I managed.) When he goes out to inspect the camp I quickly make my toilet and tidy my bedding by the stove and attend to any other matters of personal care, such as I might have. This is the only time of day during which he is reliably absent and I can see to these things. I have reclaimed some of my modesty; there is a water closet here, a fairly new one, a blessing so huge it makes me want to praise heaven. It's tiny, once the door is closed there is hardly room to use it, but it gives me a little dignity. And him too I suppose. There is no running water in the schoolhouse—just a well in the yard—but a separate pipe leads from the well to the building, and through the wall to the high tank in the closet. Every morning I go out and pump the handle to fill the tank with water. I had never seen such an arrangement before; I don't think I could ever have imagined it myself. I assume that some missionary teacher insisted.

After that I clean his bedroom. It's colder there, though still warmer than the out-of-doors, and I am surprised that he would give me the more comfortable place. But perhaps he really is from the north, as I've pictured him. He strikes me so. Hokkaido is a long way from here, a long way north, and though an island it must be wintry in the depths of the season. He may prefer the cold. At any rate he must have that room to himself and the only way to change it would be to move the stove, which is old and heavy and might go to pieces, and even then they would have to make a hole for the chimney. Not that I am sorry; it is all to my benefit. I love that stove as I once did my mother. I want to stay with it forever.

He usually returns while I am still in his room but he sits down at the table in the other while I finish. He may work then or he may stare out the window. He always speaks when I come through but it is never very much, most often a pleasantry, sometimes a question I don't want to answer or want to answer falsely. When I am done with his bedroom he generally goes into it but for the rest of the day he is here and there, back and forth between the rooms and in and out the door, watching me closely at times and at others not at all, occasionally talking to me. I reply but we have no real communication. I think he would like me to improve my Japanese but he does nothing to assist this.

It is a peculiar kind of life. Not very different after all. I was surviving day to day, minute by minute, every hour, and now I do a little more but it is also just the same.

He asks about my parents, asks about them every day. I can't go on ignoring it so what should I tell him? Their names and dates of birth? Their dining habits, their heights and weights? Or something more personal, more revealing—that they were oddly matched, the doctor and his unschooled wife, that I did not understand their attachment? That they wanted different daughters and I was caught between the two? That the first thing I remember is trying to be my father's child and the next my mother explaining to me, "Because I am a woman and you are still a little girl," and feeling certain she was right?

Anything but what he really wants to know.

He doesn't often have his men in but sometimes he does. When it is me, or me and him, I go about my duties lightly, even contentedly; there is not that much to do and I like cooking, I like cleaning, I like sweeping and washing the bedclothes (though not the uniforms) and even scrubbing the floor, because it makes my home here better. I don't like going into the yard—I am reluctant to expose myself—but this is only for short periods. Then I am back inside.

But when the men are here I hate it. They watch me, I can hardly move a step. I want to hide in the toilet or run away. I go on about my work but it is a different thing then. There is nothing to console me.

Within the confines of his chambers I am secure, though, most of the time, and comfortable. Because I very rarely leave them I can make myself a world. I am well off and in a way I don't think it has entirely to do with wartime, or hunger or cold, or fatigue, or even fear; there is something about a limited existence that lends dimension to one's thoughts, a manageable quality, the termination of desire. Not that I had a shred of desire left in me—not that I had anything left in me, I can still feel the numbness there like a hardened lump of flesh, a piece of woman turned to steel—but who's to say I couldn't have abandoned it even if I had? Who's to say I might not have settled as easily, as naturally into such a life without the Japanese, without the war, without all this destruction and the suffering and terror? Was there not enough to be afraid of in the world before they came? Not enough misery? Not enough doubt? At some moments, as I crouch and look out the window at the dull and aching fields, I think I have been waiting for something like this all my life. For a reason to cut my universe down to a circle forty paces wide. And at its center, me.

But I also stay inside because of circumstance, it's true. Because of history. I stay because I have no reason to leave but also because I have many reasons not to. I stay because I am tired, because I am blunted, because I'm afraid to be away from him, afraid to even be seen by the soldiers. And I cower when he is gone, though most often I'm not aware of it. He kept them from me once, yes, and probably will again. And they all know who I am, they know what happened (perhaps they aren't certain it was me he saved, but they know he saved a Chinese girl and brought one back with him), and while I imagine they don't think he actually values me, actually cares about my welfare—there are so many like me, after all—I am a possession of his and they would not harm me any more than they would harm his boots or his books or his supper bowl. He is their officer. But I am desperately afraid of them; I know a part of what they've done. And I know what armies are. I know enough of what I need to know, what I need to be reminded of.

The fact is they are fighters, young men in mass. If they weren't beast soldiers they would still be frightening; if they hadn't torn my country apart I would still take extra care. If I didn't know what these particular young men had done not long ago—let us say they are all innocent, that by some kind of luck or celestial design he was given a corps of the only decent, honorable, law-abiding soldiers in the emperor's Asian army—I would fear what they might do tomorrow. Any woman would. They are fighters, triumphant warriors, and know that women are their spoil.

Where the largest armies are I know arrangements have been made. In Manchuria and Korea I'm sure they keep them entertained, and in Peiping and Shantung, and also wherever Kuroda's comrades have gone, at the end of the trail the long black snake was carving over the dusty hills that day. But these soldiers are alone and must create their own amusements. It is different here, this is not the conquered city—this is another place and another moment—but I consider myself at risk.

He is not entirely like his men. It is hard to see him as a Japanese at some times, hard not to at others. His eyes change. One day he is of them and the next of himself. I know nothing about him. I don't know who he really is. If I had some idea of his job, even, of his street address, of the name of his wife, of his favorite toy when he was small, I could better gauge him. I could be more certain of him, of this man who preserves me. When I wondered about next month, next week, tomorrow afternoon, I could risk at least a guess.

But I am coming to know him despite myself. I live in his home, or he in mine. We are constantly together.

What is disturbing about his smell is that it reminds me of so much. It is the smell of a man. It reminds me of my father—though I struggle against this—and of my brother, and of my husband. It is the smell of a man and it sickens me that such a smell could still have meaning, could still have presence in my life and not be smashed down into pieces like everything else that once was whole. What with rape and slaughter and invasion and slavery you would think that nothing would be human anymore, nothing would be the same, that categories and connections would be shattered and erased and give way to random moments, random crises, random pains. Who is this man to smell like my husband? What of it that they're both men? My father was a doctor and my brother a doctor's son and my husband a merchant and this man is who knows what and a Japanese soldier besides, a servant of the rising sun, and they all think differently and act differently and cast a different eye so what then is shared between them? Why must they join in common, in common to pursue me?

What is infuriating is that I am trapped here. What is maddening is that it is the obvious thing, the only thing, that going on like this constitutes *making the best of it* and *surviving day to day*. What is despicable is that the whole notion of deciding, the very idea, has been held down and buggered, just like thousands of my sisters, just like China itself, by this savagery, by war, by the baseness and brutality and pointlessness of it all. In a war you don't have choices; you can't see an inch beyond your belly. There is no reason for your actions, no rhyme to your will, no meaning behind your location in space. You are worse than a scrap on the wind or a worthless coin, less than a looted opium pipe claimed in a game of cards. Despite yourself you recall for a moment, just a moment, your former life, the life that made you real, and then you remember the ragged corpses by the road, the ghosts outside the western gate, and you think: that could be me. I could be those. And you know well what you are.

I am trying very hard but I can't try hard enough. I am doing my best and I can't see an ending. I know, that is the war; I know, that is history. But what is impossible is that all my pride, all my dignity must now be conceded, must be cast aside if I am to outlive this, that I must surrender everything. What is intolerable is that my life, my culture, my very person must be given away. It isn't fair. It isn't decent. I have food to eat now and a nest by the stove but no possibility of any faith in who I am. Of expressing even a word of what I feel. I cannot talk to him; I can't even look at him; I cannot allow myself to follow a single true impulse when he is near because I might show him my essence, what I really think of it all, and that is unacceptable risk.

I thought I knew what hopelessness was. I thought I saw it every day in the fields and at the market and on the road to the mine, and I sighed and was glad it wasn't me. But now I know more; I am fully informed. They have taken the world away and all the old rules have been changed. Here I am and here I stay and I am bereft, I am defenseless, I have been through so much and now I'm expected to be *civil* to this man, just because he isn't going to rape me. The insult—it is hard for me. It is very hard. A month ago I would not have cared, I would not have been able, but I am stronger and healthier now and more in the nature of myself—by his hand, that is the worst of it—and it is something I can barely abide. Just barely so. As if he orders and forbids me to be human, all at once, and I am frozen in response. What other answer could I have?

We won't go on this way, I see. It's not a stable situation. I know that sooner or later, something will change it; I know some spirit will decide.

NINE

We make our quarters in the schoolhouse; it is the only decent building. It is on a low hill and has a good view of the area, and it is isolated, with almost nothing else nearby except the cultivated fields. Just to the east there is a group of twisted trees and beyond that there was once a shed of some kind, a shelter from the summer sun, but I ordered it pulled down. It is almost absurd to think it could have constituted a danger—just a rickety rotting shed not big enough for two infantrymen with their field kit on—but it seemed the prudent thing to do. Standard procedure in any case.

Suzuki claimed to have found this camp for us. He was so pleased when he told me. For all I know it was the general's staff, not him, but he insisted that he'd ordered a search on my behalf. I thanked him and told him it was excellent, which is true. It is some distance from the village but that is mostly an advantage. There is a generous supply of clean water. The building is heated by coal stoves and is comparatively airtight; there is nothing else like it inside the town or out. I am certainly more comfortable than I was when I lived in the open, before the regiment went north.

The men sleep in the classrooms, and also in tents. There are too many for the schoolhouse and I have ordered a rotation. Heaven knows if it will work but in any case the nights will be warmer soon so it hardly matters. Because this is a school and I am surrounded by young men I think often of my own school days and of lessons, of crowds of schoolboys everywhere. It is a pleasant kind of thought but it fills me up with pity; it reminds me of a picture I once saw of an estate in Canton, where the imperial examinations were given. There were rows and rows of testing cells, small brick booths with slanted roofs. It is partly the tents that remind me of that photograph, I think; they are lined up like the cells and similar in their regularity. The text said that Hung, leader of the Taiping, had repeatedly failed his examinations there. It was the strain of these failures that led him, apparently, to his visions (he thought he was God's brother) and to his violent crusade.

It is quiet in this place. There is little for me to do, little for the soldiers to do, and this presents a certain danger. I try my best to keep them occupied. If I thought it possible I would employ them in some useful manner, in rebuilding what is damaged or even making something new, but I know they would not tolerate it. I suppose that is what the Germans would do; their propaganda and their politics are very advanced. We, of course, would hardly stoop to help these people in any way, it would shame us—they are the vanquished, after all, not our equals—and if we did they would be mystified. They are not like Europeans; they are wholly unaccustomed to receiving help from anyone. In the cities there is a pretense of service (at least for the affluent and the foreigner) but not here. Here there is abuse and exploitation of the powerless by the powerful, from all walks of life—functionary, landlord, usurer, bandit—without regard to any loyalty or sense of affiliation. As frightful as we are I imagine it does not surprise the peasants, not entirely. They are used to being robbed.

From what I've gathered in the past and what I now see for myself I am amazed that nothing has happened yet, that they have not risen up together. What goes on in this land is horrendous and there are enough of them to turn the very mountains upside down. But the same few have always ruled the very many, riots and rebels notwithstanding, and I wonder if this will ever change; even their bloody anti-communist war was endlessly inconclusive, and now the whole issue seems to have disappeared entirely. Of course it would not have mattered anymore, because we have come. They can go on hurting and killing each other as long as they respect our authority; we have no desire to actually govern but we will keep a certain order. *We are under no obligation to save them from themselves*. Perhaps when we leave in a generation or two they will have learned something from us, perhaps gained some perspective. If not they can take it up as before.

How beneath me this is. How distressing to feel this way. It is the tedium and the uselessness that have turned me into so coarse and nasty a creature, I think, into a smug, small-minded man.

This is how I spend my time: I sleep. I inspect the troops and their barracks and tents and their uniforms and weapons and the radio and the kitchen and the stores and the latrine and the truck and the horses and motorcycles. I survey the territory. I eat. I go to the village periodically to be sure the people there still fear me. I question the sergeants closely about what the men have been doing. I discipline the men. I take hours to write wordy but pointless reports indicating that nothing worth noting has happened since we came here. I wonder why they need a captain (even an inferior captain like myself) to do this; I think about ordering Lieutenant Nagai to stay and setting off to find the army. I read old letters from my wife and try to answer them. I host the sergeants and the lieutenant; I hear the complaints they bring from the men, and tell them stories, and listen to theirs. I drink tea. I make a strong, smiling corporal from Shimonoseki, very tall, drive me around the countryside, he on the motorcycle and I in the sidecar, looking carefully about me (but for what I do not know).

I suppose I am childish. My situation could be worse. The two things I have never been able to tolerate are boredom and abandonment—having nothing to do and having been left behind. That is how my father would punish me: he would prevent me from spending an evening or a day in any meaningful fashion, would deprive me of my toys and later my books and make me sit in misery (or contemplation as he called it). He would refuse to take me with him when he went to Tanaka Masao's house, or to Inouye Hideo's, or to sports matches or the fisheries or to kite flying in the park. And now they have subjected me to both of these things, to my most familiar torments. I have been left behind here, left behind to do nothing—to "contemplate," to stare at the walls, to watch the days slowly lengthen. I am without diversion of any kind; I am literally without my books, except the few I have managed to keep with me, now reread so many times, and a few more I begged from the officers' library before they hauled it away, without pastime or real employment or even worthwhile conversation. It would be difficult for anyone but it is very hard for me. I must not suffer dully; I must remember why it strains me. That is how I can get through it.

And even then I have to ask: to what end, this getting through? I want to know, what is the purpose? Facing my own weaknesses is all very well but the fact is that I do not know why we are here, why I am. Really, that is the largest problem. I have received no instruction and fail to see the utility. What could happen? We must be the smallest garrison in China, what do they expect us to do? I feel they are misusing me; I feel I was carried from my home, from my family and work, to be brought here to do nothing useful, nothing proud, nothing of any description at all except be horrified and beaten down and made ashamed of my countrymen, and question the Emperor. If I must put up with all of this and be corrupted in this way I should be helping somehow. If there are Chinese to be killed, if that is inevitable, then I should be killing them. Instead of sitting in a schoolhouse wasting time. I want to make a contribution, to be a part of the war; I want to build or to destroy, to fight or to retreat, but not to stay forever in this meaningless place. I haven't even the dignity of being under fire.

The girl is mostly silent; I can't look to her to help me. I had thought for a time that she might be of interest—that our relations might help to distract me on occasion—but I sense she wants no part of me. I would talk to her more but it is clear she doesn't like it. I am grateful for her presence, she does a good job and the sight of her relieves the sameness, is even pleasant, but that is the extent of it.

I am curious about her; it would be hard not to be. I admit I am intrigued. How did she come to be lying in that yard? How did she even stay alive until that morning? Strangely, I find that having her here, wondering about her, doesn't lead to deeper interest in the Chinese all around me, as I once feared it might. My feeling for her is not transferred; I can regard her as a person without caring for the others. She is here with me, next to me, and they are down in the village and out in the fields. I never rescued them from soldiers. They are in no sense mine.

But Li is something different and I do want to know her. I want to know about her. I wish she would tell me. I ask questions and she says "yes" or "no" or stares and turns away, pretending not to understand, or she lies. I can tell when she is lying. I don't think it so unreasonable of me to want to have some answers. She is not my servant, after all, she is my prisoner, my slave; I could compel her to be truthful.

I asked her once about her family, about what happened to them. Where they were and how they were killed (I don't know that they were, not for certain, but I infer it). She would not say. I really want to hear about this; I wish she appreciated my sincerity. There is an obvious conclusion with upsetting implications but of course it could have been anything, couldn't it? I don't even know what month or year she left home. I don't know when the trouble came. It could have been our people, yes, but it could also have been outlaws, it could have been riots, it could have been a Yangtze flood a long time ago. It could have been Chiang's troops or Chu Teh's or someone else or even nature that brought them down. It could have been disease or starvation, people are always starving here. And if it was our men, what was it? The looting of their village? Caught in the cross-fire? Bombs dropped right on top of them? Some sort of unintended harm?

I don't see why I should feel a special guilt over her situation, why I should add her life to all that for which I am responsible. The burden is heavy enough; she is only one of many. Why should I concern myself if she will not even tell me? And I am helping her now. She eats my food. She is warmed by my coal. She is safe with me, very safe, safer probably than she has ever been from the day she was born.

We are such a peculiar phenomenon, she and I, it is hard to comprehend. What fate or weirdness brought us here? If we talked we could share our thoughts at least. We could speculate, we could try to guess. But she is loath to share any more than she must and it is natural for this to be so, I admit. I am not even certain that I want to share myself.

So I have nothing. I have nothing. This is punishment for me, it is a sentence to be served. With every hour that passes I get farther from recovering myself, from being Kuroda, from being whole; with every day I am less able, I think, to heal in some real way the damage I have suffered, to escape the sights I've seen. I am shattered and deprived and I am getting ever sadder. As time goes by the world shrinks closer to this building and this yard and these tents and plains and valleys, and Japan gets harder to reach, harder to imagine; I lose the meaning, even the knowledge of the center of my psyche, of my soul, of my anchor, of the essential concept *home*.

TEN

The whole camp is in an uproar. The village too. I know because I was there this morning, at the market. He sent me with a soldier to buy certain things, certain spices and ingredients; he wanted me to make something different for his meal. "I am feeling very dull," he said. "Cook me something of interest." I said he might not like what we liked in Kiangsu and he looked at me as though I were an idiot, so I suppose the sarcasm was lost on him. I said I would have to go to town for more supplies and he just looked at me and I said I was afraid and he said he would order the corporal to take me. "Yes," I said, nonsensically, and he said, "Listen, this man is very trustworthy. You will under no circumstances be harmed."

The communists seem to have blown up the bridge. The

one that crosses the river at its narrowest point, a mile and a half from here. No one saw them do it but I know it was them; the government soldiers would never dare to try it. They must have come around midnight, under cover of the storm. Though small and old it is a very useful bridge—the main road goes right over it, the only way south—and this is a serious blow. They will no doubt repair it very quickly but I'm certain they are shaken. I'm certain they are angry and at least somewhat alarmed.

The townspeople have surely taken notice as well. I was waiting to buy some pickled radishes, first off—to my amazement the market is not badly stocked and many things are available, at least in small amounts, to those who have the money—when I saw the radish vendor whispering to another woman, and the family at the stall across from hers talking quietly among themselves, and several boys and young women moving quickly from one table to the next, from one group to another. I could tell they were spreading some sort of news. At first I was offended that no one had approached me—how dare they leave me out of it?—but then I remembered the corporal I had come with, so freakishly tall for a Japanese, standing a few feet away, and the fact that I was a stranger. Even in better times we would not have spoken to a stranger in our own market, in my hometown. I might have, and certainly my father, but hardly anybody else.

"What is it?" I asked the radish woman. "What's happened?" She looked briefly at Yawata. "He can't understand you," I told her. "Don't worry."

"Three cents," she said briskly. "Three cents for the radishes."

"Answer me," I said.

Startled, she looked into my eyes for a moment, and I think she understood then who I was; she saw my father behind me, standing by his handsome house, and my husband in his suit and our apartment in Shanghai. But even so she hesitated. Normally she wouldn't have thought of showing me disrespect but there was my huge enemy soldier, looking at some gingerroot, his rifle on his back. And she could see that I was decently clothed and fed.

"You could be spying for them," she said, clutching the leaf-wrapped radishes tightly, with a dirty hand. "You could be in their pay."

To my surprise I wasn't angry. I actually laughed. "I'm not, I'm their captive," I said. "I'm their slave. But whatever it is they'll find out anyway. I'm not a spy but you know that someone is." I gestured around us. "Everyone else here has heard the news by now, including the spies. So why not tell me?"

She looked into my eyes again, for several seconds; her tattered fur vest gave off a bad smell. Her face was entirely unmoved, still cold and rigid, but then I heard her sigh ever so faintly.

"The bridge on the river was blown up in the night," she said. "They wrecked it with explosives. They got clean away."

"I hope," I said, pleasantly, "that you sell a lot of radishes today, and every day this month." She seemed puzzled. "Here is twenty cents," I said. She shook her head.

"I don't have seventeen cents," she told me.

"I don't want seventeen cents," I said. "I mean for you to keep it. They've stolen plenty of our money, why shouldn't I give some back?" She studied me, then took the coin and handed me the radishes. "But be generous with the others," I said.

"Do they hurt you?" she asked.

"Not so far," I said.

I could see as I shopped for the rest of what I wanted, my escort tagging along behind, frightening everybody, that there was nothing else to tell. Whatever had been done had been done without the townspeople, so there were no insiders to trade on their knowledge. Or if is there were they were keeping it quiet. Probably some farmer's wife had seen the ruined bridge at dawn and had told her husband, who had brought it into town with his duck eggs or his grain. Now everyone knew and there were no facts to fuel the discussion, just speculation. Who did it, they asked, and how, and why *our* bridge, why not the railroad? To provoke the invaders? To foil some enemy plan? I overheard their questions, perhaps because they meant me to. And what will the officer do about it? they asked. Whom will he punish? How angry will he be?

When I first heard that it distressed me terribly. It simply hadn't occurred to me that there would be reprisals against the populace, that he might order them; it hadn't occurred to me, for all it was obvious, because it was so unpleasant and difficult to think about. Because I had refused it. I stood fingering the dried peppers I had just bought, at a premium—they were old, it is true, but they must have come a hundred miles or more at some point, who would have thought to find them in that filthy little market in the middle of a war?—and considered the likelihood. I will have to do something then, I thought. I will have to become brave. I realized that part of me had been childishly pretending that

I was through with tribulation, that this horrible time of ours was like a wildfire in the fields that burns its way around you, over you, and never returns, something you suffer only once (though you live among the ashes). That it was simply a matter of patience, of waiting and seeking peace. I knew very well that this was not the case but some portion of me had believed it. Hearing the word *punish*, though, that horrid word, brought me fully to my senses, flooded my mind with all the ugly possibilities I'd carried with me every day as I was scavenging through the countryside, sleeping in the dirt, that made it easy for me to banish my humanity and live as a walking and eating machine. You should be like that now, I told myself, you should never have changed back; it is the only way to be. But I wasn't convinced. I was terrified instead. The more I strained to stop caring the more frightened I became.

After that I concluded my business very quickly. I wanted to be away from the rest of them as soon as I could. As I put the last purchase into my bag I looked around for the corporal; I panicked for a moment when I couldn't find him anywhere. Then I saw him, a few yards away, examining some jellied river eels. I started toward him—I almost called out in Japanese and had to shut my mouth—but I stopped to watch him and also the eel woman. Her forehead was very high and she seemed dignified to me; there was a substantial air about her clothing and her clean gray hair, combed and neatly tied. She was standing very still, her gaze at his feet, but as I watched she suddenly stepped forward with her wooden tongs and plucked an eel from the jar. She held it out to him. He looked at her; his face was extremely stiff. Everyone nearby was watching them. He was far the tallest person in the market. The woman moved the eel a little closer to him, maybe an inch, and then he stepped away and waved his hand quickly back and forth, his fingers up and his palm to her. "No, I don't want it," he said sharply in Japanese. The woman was paralyzed. She didn't know what to do. She held the eel out, dripping its jelly. He waved his hand at her again; he was confused and annoyed. "I don't want your rotten eel," he told her.

"Please, Corporal Yawata, let us go back to the camp," I said in Chinese as I approached him. He turned to me when he heard his name, relieved but still annoyed, still upset. My hands were trembling. "Please," I said to him in Japanese, "go now." With that he started walking rapidly toward the market gate, his strides enormous, pushing to the ground a young boy who stood in his way. I followed as quickly as I could. I knew their eyes were on to my back as I went. And on his rifle. I wanted to spin and shout at them, to rant as if a lunatic. I wanted to warn them or scold them, something urgent and direct, but I had no specific message. Just a strong desire to shout.

The corporal and I walked silently up the road. The ground was soaked from the overnight rain. In some places the footing was very difficult, especially because I was reluctant to ruin my only pair of shoes, or lose one entirely in the deep mud. I was careful to remain a safe distance behind him. I didn't want to make him angry. He looked back several times, with a clouded expression.

When we arrived at the schoolhouse it was clear that they knew. The sergeants were shouting at the men and some sort of party was forming up. I stood in the yard by the well amid all the activity, looking for Kuroda, but I couldn't see him anywhere. I was even more frightened than I had been before. I started for our quarters, hoping he was in them but knowing he wasn't. As I neared the door Corporal Yawata moved into my path. The lieutenant was with him, a very ugly man with steel glasses and bad brownish skin, and he grabbed my arm and made me stop.

"What did they say in the village?" he asked. "What did they say about this outrage? Who did it?"

"Can't speak," I told him. "Can't speak."

He slapped me. "I know you speak Japanese," he said. "You speak it well enough to understand my question: *who attacked the bridge?*"

I closed my eyes. My face hurt. "I don't know," I said.

"Liar." I waited for him to slap me again. "Who was it?"

I took a deep breath. "Lieutenant, sir, no one in the village knows who did it," I said. "At least no one who spoke to me. And other than this morning I haven't ever left this camp. I have no way of knowing, Lieutenant, sir."

I could smell him leaning close to me. "Stop your lying," he said, but less angrily. He paused. "What were you doing in the village, anyway?"

I opened my eyes to find his disgusting fungus face just six inches away from me, peering closely at mine. "The captain sent me," I said. "To buy these things." I thrust my bag in front of me, forcing him to step back. He raised his hand.

"Is that so, Corporal?" he asked of the other.

"Yes, sir," said Yawata. "The captain ordered me to take her."

"She spoke to the garbage in the village, didn't she?"

"Yes, sir," said Yawata. "But not very much. And I was always nearby."

The lieutenant laughed, or rather snorted. "Always nearby," he said with contempt. "Always nearby. You get back to your squad." He turned his rage-filled eyes on me and I wanted to sink to the ground. "Someday he'll get tired of you," he said, very softly, so the corporal wouldn't hear as he marched away. "Now go inside and stay there, you Chinese whore. Understand?"

I hurried to our quarters as fast as I could. I slammed the door behind me. Kuroda was not there but some paper and a pen lay scattered on the table, and I could tell that many feet had been in and out because the floor was a mess. I shivered as I unpacked my bag, though the stove was warm. He had promised me the pick of whatever we could find in the kitchen that night, whatever meat might be available—he had been most excited about his feast—but I thought it would probably be postponed. I hadn't purchased anything that wouldn't keep. I carefully placed each item in a jar or a bowl or basket and put them all up on the cooking shelf, next to the plates and the pots and pans.

I wonder if he will retaliate. I haven't stopped wondering. It is entirely up to him. I can't honestly say that I know, one way or the other. I don't even feel that I can make a guess. And I can't possibly imagine what I'll do if he does. That kind of future is beyond me.

It would be the appropriate thing, I think, given his position. Not that it would stop them from striking again, but I know it is standard Japanese procedure—standard procedure for any occupying army, I would imagine—to kill civilians in reprisal. At Tientsin, after all, they destroyed the university with bombers because of an uprising, because some Japanese soldiers and merchants were attacked. And then they bombed the tenements, the poorest quarter of the city, though the people there were never a part of it. So why wouldn't they kill a few peasants in response to this sabotage? Why shouldn't they? They don't care. The only proper thing for him to do would be to go down to the town, assemble the people, read a statement about the bridge in Chinese—my god, he might make me do it—and shoot a dozen of them dead. And hang their heads on a wire across the road.

But I don't know him well enough; I don't really understand him. Something tells me I may be surprised. Yes, it's what he should do. It's plain and easy to decide. But what does that suggest, for a strange man like him, for an imperial misfit? For a scholar far from home?

I'm dreaming. He will. Of course he will. And I don't know what I'll do, what I'll do if he does. Should I insist he start with me?

After I put the food away and cleaned the floor I sat down by the window, to look out and rest my feet. The camp was quiet. The rain that had been threatening, that had never really left, had finally started again. The sky was black and the water dashed against the glass. I thought of Kuroda down at the river in the downpour, examining the bridge, thinking over the possibilities. I saw his grim face as he considered its repair. And I thought also of the guerrillas who had blown it up, whoever they were, wherever they were hiding: lying in the mud under the bushes or beneath a rice bin, eating their biscuits, remembering the bright flash and the bitter smoke and the sound of the explosion almost lost in the thunder, feeling their power, missing their loved ones, waiting for the darkness in which to make their way back home.

ELEVEN

This is my responsibility. It should never have happened. It is what they were expecting when they put us in this place and I should have anticipated it; I should have prevented it. That was my duty. Now it has happened and my duty is to respond, to decide what is best and to act. To rebuild the bridge, of course. At least the men will have something to do! Fortunately it is not badly damaged. But further—to guard it nightly thereafter? To search for those responsible? To take action against the villagers, as both punishment and warning?

I don't think I will retaliate in the most extreme fashion. I don't believe I can. I could not care less about the townspeople and I know what I should do—what am I here for if not to punish?—but I fear my men, I am afraid to get them started. I cannot bear to watch it happen again all around me. What if they get a taste of blood? What if they get a taste of rage and pleasure? These men were standing over Li in the farmyard. *These men were in Nanking*. It has been difficult to limit their behavior so far and I have depleted my authority in doing so—there is not a man in the camp who is unfamiliar with the story of how I stopped them from assaulting her, and does not find it contemptible—and if something sets them free I will lose them entirely. I will not be able to control them. Only by showing the greatest consistency—by being so odd in my treatment of the Chinese as to be considered demented, but fully logical all the same—can I hope to keep them in check. I know I *should* kill the villagers, but would I? As far as the soldiers are concerned? If I admit to being one of them I can never take it back.

Certainly my fears are exaggerated, yes, even hysterical. I know this. They are just farm boys and factory workers, after all, and what happened before was extraordinary. The elements were commonplace but the endless frenzied repetition, day after day after week, was a particular phenomenon that is unlikely to recur. It happened that way because the highest generals allowed it or even desired it and because the rations were short, and the whites high-handed, and the battle for Shanghai so long and brutal and wearying. Because the soldiers of the capital ran or gave themselves up, like indolent traitors, instead of honorably defending it. If I were not their commander these men would be mistreating the people here, certainly, in one way and another, but it would not be as it was. Even the meanest private does not wish for that again.

But still. It is sensible to be afraid. And I am afraid. It was the worst thing I have lived through; I cannot bear to take the risk. I cannot bear to act out a part of it again, even the tiniest part, no matter if it is my duty, while my soldiers stand and watch me in the muddy village street.

And there is even better reason to exercise restraint. It may be militarily right—I know it is militarily right—but it is very, very bad, to punish the innocent. I do not wish to be a party to it. I never have in all my life, I do not want to start now, I do not want to go home (if I ever go home) with that, too, buried in me. I have come so many miles without crossing any borders, without abandoning my soul; I want to stay true, if not clean, if not pure.

I could have been part of it. It would have been easy. I could have joined the others during those dim winter days and those long winter nights: burning, killing, looting, maiming, raping, raping, raping. I could have given in. I shot at Chinese in Hopeh and Chahar because they were shooting at me; I cheered our gunners in Shanghai because they were hunting down those who were trying to destroy us; but I have yet to harm a prisoner, I have yet to touch a woman, I have yet to steal, torture, desecrate, murder since I came to this country. My forbearance has done *them* no good whatsoever but it is all I have left, my only remaining treasure and my basis for staying whole. Have I carried myself safely through that rotten stinking mire, through all that degradation, to allow a single charge of dynamite under ancient stone and mortar to corrupt me all at once, to push me to the other side?

But I am forced to do something. I have recognized the need.

Partly I am mortified and ashamed; partly I am frightened. Also I am angry. I am outraged. There is a small Kuroda in me who sees it is ridiculous but I am genuinely furious that they should have such effrontery. How dare they? Who do they think they are? They are so prideful, these people, though their country is debased, though we have beaten them over and over again and always prove they cannot fight. The last time was just four decades ago. My father was here. I myself can remember the Twenty-one Demands and their quick capitulation. It made an impression on me, because I was old enough to understand; there was nothing they could do, I saw, for all their numbers and their arrogance. We have beaten them and the whites have beaten them, they are poor and unproductive, it has been centuries since they meant anything, ruled anything, did anything other than breed and swarm and starve, and still they think they are better. Still they think they can fight us. *We have killed them by the hundreds and the hundreds of thousands and still they come out in the darkness and destroy a tiny bridge.*

When I found her in my quarters, sitting silent by the window, I asked her who it was. I felt I had to try. She looked up at me and said: "How would I know?" I waited and stared right back.

"You will not tell me," I said. "I understand."

She knelt. "I do not know," she said, as she removed my muddy boots. "Do you understand that?"

Revelation: there are things I don't know, things I should have known. Things I would have known, if I were like the rest of them. Training I never got because I was not at the Academy. It is clearer to me now. I have despised the others for their narrowness, their bigotry and cruelty, their ignorance, but I have forgotten how well they can do the work that I cannot. I have been sitting like an idiot when there are steps I could have taken. The recruitment of spies. Random night patrols. Searches of the countryside for evidence of partisans. I have been scratching at the rudiments of these, I suppose, enough to fool myself and to satisfy the lieutenant (though he must think me hardly competent) but I have done it very badly. I have acted like a senile daimyo of my father's grandfather's generation, riding out to gaze upon my land and my peasants, instead of the commander of a minuscule encampment in an enemy country in a world with explosives and mortars and bombs.

I AM ILL-PREPARED FOR THIS.

Suzuki will criticize me. I should instead chastise him, it is he who left me in this mess, but he will make his snide remarks. He will protect me but he will scold. I feel helpless and juvenile, without defense or justification. It is true, it is most of all Suzuki's fault—he should have known I was not ready for this duty, he should have left me with better orders—but also, in a larger way, I have been overlooked. It is puzzling. I am very much abnormal and there is no provision for me, there is no way for them to compensate, but why then would they have selected me for this role? Me of all people? As I search for explanations I conclude that they lost track of me. They must have. I no longer carry a label; they have forgotten who I am.

No matter how you try to live they will humiliate you. It is inevitable. If there is a way in which you might fail they will find it and expose it. And there will be such a way; they will see to that too.

Listen, Major: I will not be surprised again. I will not be

uninformed. After inspecting the bridge and doubling our guard I approached Lieutenant Nagai about recruiting local agents. He speaks not only the language but even the dialect they use here, more than well enough to be understood. And this assignment suits his temper. He will make regular trips to the villages and the farms, under cover of night, well-supplied with money and promises and threats, to find those who can help us. He will address them one by one. He seems to relish the prospect; I suspect he has been waiting for me to give the order. I will not be surprised again.

The real problem is the railroad. I had considered it but not at length. I had judged it out of my jurisdiction, too far away, but it is the obvious target. And there is no one else to protect it, not for miles up and down the line. I must think about it now. I am overwhelmed by my responsibilities but I suppose I must start somewhere; there is nothing else to do. We cannot possibly patrol the railroad and that is why we must have spies. Not only as informants but as guards where we cannot guard, eyes where we cannot see. I don't think we could repair the slightest damage to the tracks. We would have to send for help. That is why we must anticipate. We must prevent it from occurring.

After we discussed the future gathering of intelligence I had Nagai compose a brief message, in Chinese, to be posted in the village. I asked him to assemble the people and recite it to them. It warns of the severest possible action to be taken against anyone who is found to be cooperating with guerrillas. It warns of extreme reprisals to be made against civilians in the event of further incidents. I asked him if it would be fully convincing and he said he thought it would. I gave a number of further instructions and sent him on his way, with a large party—in the truck, to make it all the more impressive, and with several horses too.

Then I went to find Li. I wanted to go walking, to get away from Nagai and the sergeants and the men and the machinery of war, to pretend that I was elsewhere. But I had no desire to be alone. I felt that the bombing had probably ruined forever our chances for friendship but that made no difference to me, not just then. We were on opposite sides; if she wanted to be silent she could, if she wanted to hate me she could. If she had a knife and I turned my back she could stab me—I judged myself to be fair game. But her company was the only thing within my power that I actually wanted at that moment, her face was the only human face I wished to see, and if I commanded she would obey.

She turned from the stove as I entered. "Should we go to the kitchen now?" she asked. "Then I can begin to cook your dinner."

I shook my head. "Get your coat and come with me," I said. She went to the corner and took up her ragged woolen field jacket—we'd saved it from the corpse of one of our dead at Changshu, against future need—and put it on before following me out the door.

The rain had stopped altogether but it was still a misty day as we moved west across the grounds. Ahead of us the sun was shining dully in the clouds but I did not think it would make it through before evening. Some of the men saw us going; I took care to show that I was out on business, not for pleasure. Good, I thought, now they can believe her an informant after all. Maybe they will respect me for it, or at least suspect me less, and she will be that much safer. At the edge of the field, where the smooth granite boulder sits embedded in the ground, we started together down the slope.

"Where are we going?"

"You ask a lot of questions for a prisoner."

She was silent for a moment. "You answer a lot of them," she said, "for a Japanese dwarf."

I turned angrily around but was surprised to find her smiling. Not broadly, just very slightly, but she was smiling as she walked. Apparently it was a joke. No well-bred girl would do it, it was entirely improper, but it was an effort to be friendly nonetheless. Offensive but at least personal. She chooses a peculiar time, I thought. When she reached me she stopped.

"Is that what you call us?" I asked her. "Dwarves?"

She looked at the ground, perhaps regretting her irreverence. "Among other things," she said. "You can imagine."

We started down the slope again. In the distance were the western hills, barely visible through the clouds and mist. Spread before us there was nothing but cultivated ground, with some scattered grazing areas and ponds and a few small stands of trees and shrubs. I headed directly for the largest of these. I thought there might be birds there. There was a path—I could see a path—that would take us through the fields so we could reach it.

"Please walk beside me," I said. After a moment she complied. I looked at her and saw how clean her black hair was, how smooth and bright. It surprised me. Then I remembered that she usually had it bound up in a cotton scarf, which no doubt helped her keep it shiny. I had found her by the stove without her headcloth and she had not even reached for it, had not even asked if she could quickly run and get it when I ordered her to follow.

"Does your wife walk beside you?" she asked. I looked at her again. I thought of saying, "How would I know?" I wanted to scold her for her impolite questions and her impudent jokes.

"Not usually," I said. "What of it? Did your mother walk with your father?"

"No," she told me, "but I walked with my husband."

"You are married?"

"I was."

"Is he dead?"

"He left me."

"Are your parents dead?"

She breathed deeply. "They are," she said.

We reached the edge of the furrowed fields. I could see they had been planted for the season not long before, and while one was still unrelieved dirt the other already had the smallest shoots of growing green—some kind of cereal, I guessed—just emerging from the rows. A curving footpath took us between the two (the boundaries were far from square) and we started down it. It was too narrow for us to walk together; I gestured her ahead of me. She looked reluctant but she went.

It occurred to me then that I was doing a very foolish thing. We were not out of sight of the schoolhouse, not even out of rifle range, but I was the captain, after all, a prized target. I tried to put it from my mind.

After a few steps I called to her to wait. I knelt to study the growing plants. They were barley. I pulled one out to peer at the roots, to examine them for parasites. Looking up I saw her watching me. "I'm putting it back," I said, and I did. I pressed the soil in around it, then stood and brushed the dirt from my knees. The smell of it had calmed me.

We walked without speaking for several minutes more. I enjoyed watching her from behind, the loose and easy way she moved along, her hanging head of hair. We heard only the cries of the birds, and the far-off sound of someone hammering or chopping—probably one of my own men—and the passage of the wind. (I cannot become used to the constant quiet here. It seems as if it should not be so quiet, as if it is under a spell.)

Just before we reached the grove the path opened out into a grassy space around it and we were able to walk abreast. She moved beside me right away but kept a wide gap between us, at least three or four feet. I looked the plants over; they were mostly bamboo with some others mixed in. I was surprised that there was so much bamboo left, that the peasants hadn't cut it all down long ago. Perhaps because such a large stand is rare this far north, I told myself; they don't even cultivate the shoots here. Perhaps it has significance I don't recognize. This seemed implausible but there it was, some of it eight and ten feet high, very straight and very useful. It occurred to me that it might be a good idea to send a party for it. It might even be of help in repairing the bridge.

She moved slightly closer to me. "You're a professor?" she asked.

"That's right. A botanist."

"I don't know that word."

"I study plants."

"Oh." She took a step away again, approaching the grove, and pointed with her right hand. "What is this plant?" she asked.

"That," I told her, "is a tree of heaven."

She looked at me. "Really? Is that what you call it?"

I shrugged. "It has many names," I said.

"I'm sure it does," she said. "But what is its real name?"

"What do you mean? Its scientific name? The Latin?"

"Yes, the Latin if you know it."

"*Ailanthus*."

"What a funny word," she said. "But *Ailanthus* what? Don't they all have two names?"

"*Ailanthus altissima* is the most common form." It wasn't easy for me to say. "There are others. I don't recall if there are separate species or just varieties. I think I've seen *Ailanthus glandulosa*, and *Ailanthus japonica* as well."

"But it's a Chinese plant? It comes from here?"

"That's right."

We walked on for a few seconds. A crow flapped over our heads. I wanted to ask again about her past but I did not think she would let me.

"Do you know Latin?" she asked me.

"Just a little. Mostly plant and animal classification." I coughed. "I suppose your father knew some too."

"Can you speak English?"

"Not so I can be understood. Pronunciation is very difficult. But I can read it fairly well."

She stopped and walked up to another *Ailanthus*. "It's something like a weed," she said. "It takes root everywhere and it's very hard to kill. Even as a tree it isn't pretty."

I nodded, though she couldn't see it. She was studying the

plant. "It thrives the world over," I told her. "It grows in almost any soil, resisting insects and disease. To some people it's a pest."

I heard her sigh. "How," she asked, still looking ahead, away from me, "did a plain and common weed end up with such a lovely name?"

I was standing about a yard behind her. I moved a step nearer but she did not turn. Her left hand was hanging at her side and the fingers of her right rubbed a reddish leaf between them. Her head was slightly bowed.

"Perhaps because it grows so quickly," I said. "Because it tries so hard to reach the sky, to reach to heaven."

She glanced back at me over her shoulder, for an instant.

"Or because it flourishes even there," I said.

Then she turned to face me. Her eyes were on a level with mine, and they were tranquil. And I could see that her mouth was set, firmly set but not with fear, not with anger. We were closer than we had ever been before. She looked very strong and very wise as I watched her face, as she watched mine.

"I think that I should be your mistress," she said.

I took a step—a small step—away from her. Still she watched me steadily.

"It isn't necessary," I said.

"Perhaps not," she replied.

"You might bear a child."

"No. I'm sure I wouldn't."

I turned from her and moved back toward the path. It came to me that she had assumed all along that I was bringing her to this place to seduce her—to force myself on her—

and that she was actually trying to make it easier for me, for both of us, by raising the subject. By offering herself. To spare us the unpleasantness of my onerous demands. Bizarre as this idea was I could not suppress it, and when I looked at her again there was a kindness in her eyes. It was unmistakable. It made me frantic. I wondered, what have I done to bring this on? Does she remember where she is? Does she realize what she's saying?

"I'll protect you either way," I told her.

"I know," she said.

I looked out over the fields. "My men will consider you a prostitute," I said.

She laughed and said, "They already do." Of course she was right. Another thing I had not faced.

"And those Chinese who now hate me for serving you will continue to hate me," she went on. "And your people will continue to savage my country. And the Chang Chiang and the Huai Ho will keep flooding. And the children will still starve."

The sun was low over the hills and finally free of the clouds, glowing deep red over a spreading whiteness. The breeze had picked up and the bamboo was swaying. "I should tell you," I said, pacing now, looking down, "that I sent some men into the village, just before we left. On account of the bridge. They were to warn the people there that in the event of further sabotage, civilians will be killed. They were to post notices to that effect. Then they were to go to the market and confiscate everything being sold there, and destroy it, and burn the tables and the stalls."

She looked at me. "I know that," she said.

"It isn't possible. You weren't there."

She sighed again. "I don't see how you could do differently," she said.

I was baffled. It was incomprehensible. "What is the point of this?" I asked her in earnest. I could hear the tension, the uncertainty in my own wavering voice. "Why are you summoning trouble this way?"

"Why did you stop them from raping me, then?" she asked me in return.

At that moment it was most difficult to feel safe. I looked around at the open fields and saw that we were very exposed; there could have been any number of people nearby. I thrust my hands into the pockets of my coat, hoping to find something to reassure me, to soothe me, but they were empty.

"You didn't ask me that," I told her. "You're much too bright and much too sensible. We never had this conversation. Now let's get back to camp."

TWELVE

The season is changing and I can feel it. It remains chilly, yes, and much of what we look on is still brown, but I can now believe that in a few weeks or a month the hills will be friendlier, the days more tolerant. The world will become a more welcoming place. When I was younger I often laughed at these changes, these cycles, and found them ridiculous because they were transient and trivial, in no way enduring; when the weather improved it wasn't as if it were forever, as if our circumstances were going to be permanently bettered, and when the cold and the darkness returned I found no reason to despair. It was, I once told my mother, as if the people said upon rising, praise heaven that the light is here again, and at sunset, what a tragic occasion this is. She looked at me as though I were very odd and said, but that is what I say; that is just what I say. It was a way in which we often had misunderstanding. It always seemed to me that it required absurdly little to make her smile, or make her cry.

But with age and with trouble I have a different perspective. War, I would think, gives altered borders to us all. For two months I knew—I knew—that I had less than a week, less than a day, less than a minute left in my life; for another I have looked just slightly farther ahead. Only recently have I even reached the point of expecting, when hungry, that my hunger will be satisfied. I have no vision; I do not know what will happen sooner, happen later, happen by and by, and the coming summer is an incomprehensibility spreading before me, a vast and mysterious space like the surface of the Tai Hu when I was brought there as a child. It is an obstacle, a spectacle, in just the same way. I can no more see the end of it than I could peer over that water to the opposite shore; I have no more means of crossing it than I had a boat, at the Tai, or a servant to row me.

What I am trying to say—what I am trying to accept—is that my heart, I am now old and wise enough to know, will not allow me inhumanity. It was hobbled by my fear and by my struggle, when I was hiding, it conceded to the numbness, but that concession was necessity and not permanent defeat. When I could not afford feeling I had it not; now there is room for it and it is with me again, as inevitably as the life that has returned to my bowels, now that I am fed, and the dreams that are filling my cherished hours of unbroken sleep.

But to what to be attached?—that is the question. About what may I care? I still find strict limits here. Nothing old, nothing new, nothing elsewhere; nothing distant in time or place. These things are still denied me and I'm glad that this is so. I am allowed to love my sleeve; I am permitted to be interested by the vegetables I am slicing, or by the covers of his notebooks, or the clouds in the sky; I can remember, at noon, the sounds I heard when I went out to the well in the morning, and I can wonder whether it will rain again that night.

So I am grateful for these changes, for the approach of spring. It gives me something to be intrigued by every day. It gives me the material out of which to form emotion, the fuel with which to stoke a life. To think about the grass being greener and the crops higher and the leaves bigger and the sun hotter is as exciting as it would be, in another year, another land, to imagine being friends with the prime minister one day, or writing a famous book, or playing the lead in a drama. To know that something else is coming, that this cold and awful present is not forever—that it will be succeeded by a future equally awful but warm—is like knowing, on my wedding day, that I would soon be a woman, like comprehending at thirteen that I would grow up in the end, would have a family of my own, would have a house with three doors and a garden and a cook and maybe (given fortune) a small motorcar outside.

I can also hope, as a practical matter, that for the others spring will make life easier. In this season not so many will sicken and starve. And perhaps, all over China, the mood of the enemy will improve; perhaps in the green season he will be less inclined to evil than he was in the brown.

I have made a certain offer. I don't know why. To say it even to myself brings me very much alarm. I did it quickly, without planning it; it came into my head only an instant before. "Do you want to sleep with me?" I asked. And I do not think he liked it. I would be surprised—now that I've considered it—if he didn't want to, not to force me but to have me freely; looking back I recognize that certain glance, that attention that even my husband showed once he was living with me, the interest that arises from proximity alone. But he didn't like my asking. He didn't like my even having the thought, to be precise. I may be free of the larger universe, of everything but the immediate, but he is not, and he still hopes to preserve what is decent in his life. He fears disturbance. He is determined to get through this with his history intact.

I would call it impulse, what I did, but I don't see how I could have any impulse; I don't see how I could want to do anything but do what I'm told and stay as far away from everyone as I possibly can. Nothing else makes any sense. I am interested in the sky, yes, in the birds and growing plants, in the taste of my dinner, in imagining events in Peiping or Tsingtao or Nanchang, but those are all things I can have while still remaining fully passive. This was something I *suggested*, something I *volunteered*. An event that need never have happened but for me, and I can hardly believe it did. But I can't deny it, I remember it, and as astounded as I am I have to claim possession. Yes: it was me. Apparently it was something I felt was right, was proper. Something I had a need for. Or something granted after all, but in a convoluted way, my fate but a fate that required me to pursue it. This has come to me before.

We were walking together. It was his idea, not mine, of course, and following my experience in the market and with that horrible lieutenant his summons filled me with anxiety, with all sorts of morbid fantasies, or rather expectations: he was going to kill me, he was going to attack me, he was going to make me betray my people in some way. The former I dismissed before we'd gone twenty steps—while I don't know him well I'm quite certain, by this time, that he wouldn't harm my body—but the last one seemed very reasonable, even likely. He is certainly a kind man, or in any event less cruel than his countrymen, but he is thoroughly Japanese and he is trying, it is clear to me, to properly fulfill his duty. Given what had happened I knew that might include coercing me. Still, the discovery that I trusted him, even slightly, uplifted me as we moved away from the schoolhouse, as did the prospect of a stroll in the fields at last, an open daylight walk with the one person in the whole province that could make me feel a little safe. Suddenly I was enjoying myself; I was almost lighthearted.

He asked me to walk beside him and I did as he wanted. We made some slight conversation. At one point I stupidly referred to his wife and so had to admit to a husband. I told him the truth when he asked me questions but who knows whether he believed me; everything I say could be a lie and I think he remains aware of this at all times. As would I if I were he. We went on through the fields and then we came to a grove, a bamboo grove like one of the pictures on the wall in Madame Na's house, all elaborate and vital, complex and vigorous, overgrown, all weedy. I could see it in ink or watercolor, on a scroll or in a frame. It was a strange and fantastic thing to find there, in a place in which most everything has been sacrificed to the goal of getting another stalk of wheat, another yam, another piglet each year; I thought that maybe a wild animal would come leaping out and devour us, or that the image would quickly fade back into the antiquity from which it mysteriously remained.

We walked slowly by the grove. The countryside was so empty, so quiet around us. I could feel it; I could feel its destitution, its abandonment. Despite my mood I was reminded by this of the war. Some special sense within me could reach out for miles and touch it, it seemed, and measure it, this great absence, not complete depopulation but still the subtraction from what had once been of the dead and the wounded, the immobile, the refugees and those who had escaped. It was as if Huainan had been lifted by its eastern edge and tilted and everyone drained, rolling and tumbling, into the mountains in the west. As if we had the near hills to ourselves.

We naturally talked about the plants as we looked; it turns out he is a botanist, or so he says. Though he seems able to back it up. No reason for him to invent such a thing, but it's hard for me to credit. The problem is that it creates such an idiotic picture: that of a Japanese gardener, an expert Japanese gardener, leaving Japan of his own free will to fight in a war of conquest. It isn't as though his emperor needs protecting, after all. It isn't as though he is defending his islands. And furthermore it entirely stretches and even overwhelms belief to think that I, I, could have been taken prisoner—saved and taken prisoner—by the one officer in the Japanese army who isn't an officer after all, who is not only not an officer but is instead a bewildered scholar, wandering out of his element, trained not to lead but to lecture on the activities of stem cells and pollen and on how to tell the young male gingkos from the female, to avoid the stink!

Well, he came here, for some reason or another, and he was bound to pick out someone. So many are dead, so many are maimed and hungry, and then there is me. Here with him. If it had to be someone—if it had to be a woman—she had to have a name. She had to have a childhood. She had to have a face and legs and hands and breasts. And all those turn out to be mine.

He seemed uneasy; I thought it was my presence, or perhaps the solitude. He seemed uneasy but I was very calm. The grove was like a balm to me, like medicine. It was out of all proportion. The fresh, rich air filled my lungs and the smell and the sight of the greenery, just coming out, somehow healed me. I felt, waiting by the bamboo shafts and talking with him, more solid, more intact, than I had since the bombs first started falling on Shanghai. I was invigorated. I stood there and looked at a baby chun shu—*Ailanthus*, he called it, and also tree of heaven—and thought that it would soon be much bigger, that it would grow and grow all summer, and then found to my amazement that I identified with this. That I felt once again like a living growing thing. And there came a rush of feeling about him on account of it, a sudden flood of recognition, not only that I was surviving and recovering and that he was responsible but that the conversation we were having, at that moment, was a genuine thing, that his gentleness in teaching me was something to value, that he appeared to honestly care. It wasn't as if I actually liked him, or admired him—a strange-walking, odd-featured, criminal beast soldier Japanese after all—but I felt generous. It was appropriate. He had given to me and I wanted to give to him in turn.

So I considered the question of what I had available, as we

talked; I took inventory of my person. I knew at the start that there was little there to offer. I had almost nothing left, not for him or for China, not for my parents themselves should they approach me from their graves. But there was something odd in me, I found, something more than I'd expected; I realized, as I searched myself for gifts, that that which had been taken from me, cleverly, through false and shameful pretense had been returned over time, restored by the virtue of my nature as a woman (or maybe by its burden). I was whole again and hadn't known it. Captured and endangered, yes, a step away from death, but I had let go, at last, of my husband and what he'd done to me. I was no longer the betrayed. Sensing this, I took a step out of confusion. Knowing this, knowing it truly, I made the suggestion that I did. I can't begin to say why but I see that one led to the other, surely, as the winter leads to spring.

Perhaps this world I live in now, this shrunken, barren, broken world, is just the one I've always wanted. Perhaps its boundaries make me free.

THIRTEEN

I am not what I was yesterday.

The act is unfamiliar. My body is almost new. As if what I once embraced is turning strange and distant from me, as if I had only been told about it. As if what was unimagined is now sleeping in my heart.

I want to run from her kindness .

There is a full moon tonight, full or very close to full. I can see my hands clearly as I stand by the south window. Even they are different, resting on the rough wooden sill. Even my fingers are changed. They are foreign to me. They might almost have been left with me, to safely keep, while my own were stolen away.

I am grateful for the quiet now. I have spurned it all these weeks but now I'm grateful. I could stand here all night and not be disturbed. When I hold myself still I can even hear her breathing; if I went to the open doorway I could probably just see her, curled up on the floor. If I could stop the sun from rising and the moon from moving on I could stand here forever, listening to the air in her lungs, watching my motionless hands, feeling the steady passage of my blood and remembering the texture of her hair, her skin, the awareness of her touch.

This is the kind of moment, I think, that comes or it doesn't. To each particular life. It comes but it may come too late, or too soon. Or it comes but cruelly hides itself, or wears a subtle guise. Some triumph; some escape; some even master it unknowing. And some are gravely harmed.

There are those who see it all and must make choices when it comes. I never imagined that I would be among them. Some choose very quickly; others are prevented from acting too fast. To each is given, I think, the time that is needed but no more. Some must wait, and endlessly wait, and never know for certain when their time will run out. I expect I am to be one of those.

I stood without speaking as she knelt down before me.

I am embarrassed by my own surprise; I think I knew all along. Not that this would happen—that we would be intimate—but that her presence here would change me. That she could never remain just a static detail. I am embarrassed—ashamed—because everyone else has known it from the beginning, she herself and Yawata and the other men and probably whoever was in that shack in the yard I got her from, and because they knew that they knew, where I knew but didn't know it. Because they've all been watching me.

It is true. It is true. As soon as I had her here I wished her gone. As soon as I brought her here I wondered why.

She thought she knew how to be Japanese. I told her I did not desire it. She thought she knew how to behave and how to approach me, how to please me and make me happy. She guessed at these things but it was false on her, she wore it badly, and I commanded her to stop. I asked her to stop. I asked her to do her best—if she was certain that she wanted this, absolutely certain, would she please do her best—to be herself. To be as I had come to know her.

"Does that mean that you admire me?"

"It must mean," I said, "that I feel love."

Surely nothing I have done has prepared me for what I have done tonight. Surely it is completely new. I have had no experience like this experience, nothing that informs it, except perhaps for one: the taste of unfamiliar food when I was very, very hungry. When I was hungry but did not know that I was. As I have wanted to spit such foods out I want this never to have happened; as I have been grateful for the flavor, for the sustenance, for the revelation of the senses so I am shocked beyond imagining to think that had I not had trouble sleeping that cold night I might have missed her. Had I not risen from my bed and gone out walking toward the village I would not have known her. She would have suffered and died there in the mud because some spirit touched my shoulder and woke me late, and let me dream the chance away.

We were nervous, we two. Without the lamp light it was easier. I wanted badly to see her—I wanted to see her jaw, her neck, I wanted to see her calf, I longed to see the shallow rounding of her breasts and the narrowing waist and the swell at her hip—but I was hugely relieved to look into the darkness. I could feel my open eyes. I cherished the moments before dim vision returned; I stared at the nothingness. In my joy I heard her gasp, and say my name.

Her hands were quick, her body strong. She is not small and I am not large but holding her I was vast, I was immense, and she the witness to it. We touched in every place we could and strained to find more, as if each exposure were to be covered, each solitude denied. It had been so long since I'd opened my mouth for anything other than to eat the sullen dinner or to speak the bitter word, but in the night I consumed her and she consumed me. I opened up to take her in. I worshipped the taste of her.

It seemed to go forever. I swear it went a thousand years.

My body was washed in sensation as I held her and my mind was filled with many things: leaf structure, the blanket, my dinner, photosynthesis, the river, far Japan, the open sea. But mostly her, mostly the woman. Mostly Li. Where was I but in her arms? Who was I but the man she clung to? I understood little, but what I knew I knew well.

And then I thought, near the finish, of the north as I first saw it. Before I fought in a battle, before I ever fired my weapon. Before I saw the blood. The chill north in early autumn, with all its wondering faces, its many eyes that followed me. I thought of the mountains there; I thought of walled cities. I thought of mud huts and of clustered grave mounds.

When the moment came I tried to leave her but she stopped me. "Don't worry," she said. "It can't do me any harm."

She took from me something I had gathered out of darkness, bit by bit, out of my body and my hatred, bit by bit, out of my soul, a growing spinning mass of hope and fear and longing, of gratitude, of the hurt that has fastened to me in my journeys through this desolation, of all my affections, of my dignity, of my freedom, of my one tiny, vanishing chance of reaching home alive. She carried it from me. I was in her and she reached into me and she took it, pulled at it, tenderly cradled it and banished it away. I felt her disencumber me.

In the end she went back to her bed by the stove.

I remember: the tips of her fingers on my face, on my back. The small sounds, like words, like the starts of words, like birds flying by me, like birds circling and waiting to land. Her small lips on my skin. The smell of her crevices, her treasures and her hiding places, the peculiar airy smell of her flesh and her sweat and her dirt and her clothing and everything she ate before the war came and everything she's eaten since, of her father's little surgery with its herbs and disinfectants and her mother's strange perfumes, of the horrors she's seen, of her passion for me, of her acceptance of my flesh, of my bone and my muscle as I lay in her arms. The smell of her grief and my pain. All mixing together, flowing, spreading as if her life, my life, our world were narrowed down to this one mysterious night. Narrowed and forced to adhere, and combine. As if we'd never be apart.

"By our standards you're not beautiful," I told her as I studied her, grasping her with arms extended, a windy open space between us.

"Nor by my own," she said.

I held her arms in my hands, one enclosed in each. She was smooth and very warm and as much as I wanted to keep from touching any other part of her with any part of me I wanted to promise myself that I would not let go, ever, not for any reason or reward that could be named. Her eyes were dark in the darkened room and I could see them watching me.

"But you are beautiful," I said. "You are beautiful. Why else would I desire you?"

"I am alive," she said, gently. "I am a woman. I speak your language." She reached for me. "Isn't that enough?"

FOURTEEN

What is this man to me?

I can't help but ask that. If I choose it or no he's at the center of my universe; he is my life now. Until there is some change he rules me. I can't pretend he is nothing, I can't pretend I feel nothing. What meaning is there for me in this world, except for him? What other question should I ask?

He is kind, after a fashion, and he is steady; that much I know. He shelters me. He transforms the worst things I could ever have imagined into what will be, I hope, a frightening memory one day. Not for others, for thousands of others, but for me; instead of death I have life, or a chance at life. He provides me with safety and warmth and food and even a sort of companionship. I accept these from him. He is my lover.

What is this man to me?

He is Japanese. He is alien. He is the subjugator of my people. He is a small and learned person who moves stiffly, who is in some ways endearing, a married foreign man who commands a group of men that is part of an army that has taken my country away. He is a plunderer. His line goes back for centuries. He is one with the Manchu, with the Englishman, with the Mongol beyond the wall.

And now I've bound myself to him, and maybe joined the other side.

I don't know why I did what I did. I just know that I did it. When it first came to me—when I made the suggestion—I was sure of myself and of my reasons. I could not name my reasons but I was sure of them. I knew they were there. Sense comes and goes in a war, though. A moment can alter everything. Now my confidence has vanished; since that night I have been wondering how it happened, why it happened. I have been wondering if it was truly me.

Not that I didn't enjoy it. I did. I enjoyed it very much. I feel faithless and defiled to think that it was better than it ever was with my husband, better than I ever thought it could be after the first time with my husband, but I enjoyed it. I enjoyed the exercise of an ability once removed from me, a capacity I thought I would always be denied. I enjoyed his desperate need. My importance to him. The fact of having something left. I enjoyed knowing that what his men, his fellow officers, all the Japanese in China want to abuse and degrade and rob me of was still mine, still intact, that I was giving it to, sharing it with, taking it from one of their own.

But all of that is pleasure. Pleasure, too, is altered in bad times. You continue and you struggle and survive and nothing matches anymore, not the way it used to, things like hardship and reward and balance don't mean anything. You want them to but they don't and then you give them up, because everything comes and goes as it will. You content yourself: you take what you can find, what you can find when you need it. And I have needs, I still have needs. No matter that things are so bad I stay human. The food and warmth are not enough; I need more, more of reason, more of substance to sustain me. If you can find it you take what you need.

But why this? Why do this? And what will I suffer on account of it?

Kuroda is attached to me. He is very attached. It is clear that he cares. That night he was an infant in my arms. I could feel him weeping inside. I gave him something; I granted him a blessing. Without meaning to I started or finished or fulfilled for him a thing he has wanted, has been waiting for through many years, a thing to make him what he never has been, what he is required to be. Perhaps that is what I was after, my intention—a special gift, some sort of recompense. Of a fundamental kind. Perhaps I am the only one, the only one in China, the only one in the world who could have done what I did. And heaven brought him to me, and me to him. For the purposes of justice. A salvaged life exchanged for life.

What does he mean to me now? Now that we've done what we've done?

We have spoken of it once. It is not that we have pretense—we are both aware at every moment of what we did, his eyes follow me and mine are more often on him than they were, and we have touched many times, though not for long—but we have spoken of it once. We are astonished by ourselves and by this situation and we are most content with silence. We are filled with hidden thoughts.

"I'm not accustomed to such ease," he said to me on the evening of the next day, looking up from the table where he was reading a document. I was stirring the stew in the big pot on the stove.

"Having dinner made for you?" I asked. I smiled and gestured around the room. "This comfort? These rich furnishings?"

He laughed—he actually laughed—but then was solemn again. He is always solemn. Even now he shows me very little of himself, and what he does show wears a frown.

"I have never been with anyone who welcomed it, as you did," he said. He looked away from me. "Who seemed entirely not to mind."

"I'm sorry," I said.

"Don't be," he answered. "That is not my purpose." After a moment he coughed. "I have a good marriage," he said.

I waited for him to continue.

"What I'm trying to say," he went on, "is that I did not expect it to be so simple for you. So relaxed."

I carefully stirred my stew.

"I apologize," he told me. "This is unpleasant for me, this conversation, but I want to know.

"Please, what do you want to know?"

"I want to know whether it was me. At least partly me." He paused. "Whether it was me that made it easy."

Brown liquid dripped from the end of my spoon.

"Yes," I said. "It was partly you."

He sat stiffly behind his table. The sunlight was finally fading; soon I would have to light the lamp.

"This is difficult for me as well," I said. I could hear the bubbling in the pot and I supposed that he could too. There was shouting from a sergeant in the yard.

We waited together, quiet, and the dusk came down around us as I slowly stirred. "You were married," he said.

"I was very briefly married."

"Why did he leave you?"

"Because I was barren."

He watched me. "He could have taken a lesser wife."

"That is true," I said. "But he chose not to."

He sighed and looked away from me. Then he looked at me again and I could see his gaze fall to my abdomen, and to the tops of my thighs.

"How did you know?"

"Excuse me?"

"How did you know that was the problem?"

"I had never," I said, "shown the sign of being a woman. The sign all women show." I stirred the food. "I haven't yet."

"I'm sorry," he said.

"Don't be," I told him. "Given the circumstances it's for the best. As I'm sure you agree."

To my surprise he nodded then. He seemed comforted by my admission, by my putting it that way. I had a passing vision of the two of us together in our very old age, sitting in a humble country room somewhere, nodding slowly and steadily from morning until night.

He looked down at his paper again and I lifted the cover of the other pot, to check the rice. He didn't appear to be reading but I knew the conversation was ended. For an instant I hoped he felt bad about his own thoughts, felt guilty, felt thoroughly evil—how lucky that this woman whom I want so much to lie with counts among her misfortunes the curse of infertility!—but then I was ashamed. I felt guilty myself. I know he doesn't think that way. I am sure he is genuinely sorry—about my husband's treachery, about my incompleteness, about the hellish situation that makes of these things virtues—and would have it be otherwise if he could. I think he loves me.

"What I really want to know," he said at last, looking up, holding a sheet of paper in his hands, "is whether you enjoyed it." He coughed again. "Whether you liked it." I stared down into the stew and said nothing. He waited for me to speak. Which I did not.

"Whether I forced you," he prompted, finally.

I drew a breath and looked at him. "Yes," I said. "Yes, I liked it." The light was so low I could hardly see him and I hated him for making me tell him that, for making me tell it out loud while he hid in the darkness. For denying me ordinary politeness, basic courtesy. I hated him because I couldn't say the rest of it, because he knew I couldn't say it, true as it was—that yes, he forced me. That even if I thrilled to it, even if it made me wildly happy, it was an act of violation. Of force and violation. It had to be. There was no way I could have done it wholly by choice, and he understood that. I was angry. I felt the heat spread over the skin of my face, my scalp, the whole of my upper body.

"*Beast soldiers*," I said, all at once, slamming down the rice pot cover. "*Beast soldiers*. Have you heard that? We call you that too."

Together we blushed in the gloom, in the deep solitude, miserable and alone.

I have trouble, at times, remembering or considering anything beyond the grounds of this schoolhouse. It is hard to imagine what one might call normal life. So I find it very strange to think, when I do, that despite our inescapable roles—master and slave, maiden and soldier, admirer and admired—we are merely two people, two of millions and millions, both intelligent, both healthy, a man and a woman who might have happened to be together even if the world had never shrieked and torn itself apart. What if my father had found a Japanese wife? What if he'd stayed in Japan? I might have grown up in Tokyo and been married to Kuroda, or to another just like him. We might have found ourselves in the same circumstances, precisely the same, without all these trappings—the war, the ruined nation, the leering soldiers yards away—but with the same essential problems: his desire, my dependence, his inhibition, my impulse, his arrogance, my distance and disdain. We are both adults and we might be discussing adult problems, money and the children's school and new furniture and his employer and my sister-in-law, all the while glancing covertly at each other as we do now and wondering as we do now and remembering the night and holding our tongues just as we do, stopping ourselves in time, as if the worst thing that could happen would be for us to speak honestly and truthfully about who we are and what we mean to each other. About what we might decide.

It would be a relief if he would approach me and say, "I want to have you again, come tonight," and walk away. It would be a gift to me. It would only increase my pleasure. I want him to instruct me; I want him to command me; I want him to describe to me his wishes in detail. Let my servitude be pure. He longs for what I have and it pleases me to know that, it satisfies me, and the more he admits it the more contented I'll become. If I must—and I must—then let us speak about it freely. Let us put away our pride.

I have been through this before. It is bizarre to say that but I have. My duty to my husband compelled me just as fully as my capture by this man, and it was equally demeaning. He too was my master; I tried in every way to please him. He too offered protection and a stove to keep me warm, and he too had strong desire. But they are more unlike than they are like, beyond race and background and station; in fact as far as I'm concerned they are very far apart. The difference between this man and my husband is that Kuroda wants, to my great fortune, what I can give him. What I have. That he is eager to possess me. And while I accept what he provides I did not come to ask him for it; I was not a supplicant. It is true that I am forced but I am also free, free as I haven't been, free of any necessity beyond each breath and every heartbeat, and yes, I chose this. I chose it. And I want it to go on.

But now he must arrange it so; I've done enough. I've done enough already. It is only fair for me to offer payment in my body—he really is a generous man, expecting nothing in return—but let him say it next time. Let him say it. Let him speak it out loud so I can hear him use the words. He doesn't owe me much, I know, but he owes me that.

FIFTEEN

I am not a good officer. I'm very sure Suzuki knows it. He is staying for a week as part of a circuit, he says, that includes other garrisons. He insists he would never come all this way just to bother me. "You can manage," he tells me. "You can manage very well without my interference." But he knows about the bridge; he mentioned it as soon as he had the chance. So why else would he have come? We haven't been here very long and the bombing was just three weeks ago. I don't see how his visit and that incident could possibly not have to do with one another. I don't see how he could be thinking anything other than that I failed him by allowing it to happen. I believe he knows how anxious I am.

"Too bad about the bridge," he said when we were finally alone, on the first day, just after the inspection I held for him. "Where was your intelligence?"

"It was lacking," I told him.

He peered at me. "This has been corrected?" he asked. I nodded and he watched my face. I waited for him to go on.

"Very good," he said at last, and that was all I heard about it.

But it isn't just the bridge; it isn't just the question of what I have or have not done about the countryside. If it were that and only that I would speak to him frankly. I would ask him: what do you want of me? Why have I had no assistance? Give me the men and supplies and tell me precisely what to do and I will do it, I would say. If it were simply a matter of complaining to him about being left here like this with so little knowledge, such slender resources, I would complain. I would, if I had my confidence. I would demand that he hear me.

But the truth is that almost nothing is right. The camp is presentable, yes, complete and orderly and reasonably clean—the major, at least, accepted most of what he saw—but the men are sullen and listless. Their personal habits ar deteriorating. They don't respect me and I think this is clear to Suzuki.

Even my officers are a part of this. I know they wonder, as I have, what I am doing here—why this garrison needs *me*—and it shows in their behavior. The sergeants are more attentive to the lieutenant's orders than they are to my own, and Nagai himself becomes more distant daily. He has not reported much progress with his assignment, despite what I said to Suzuki, and he tells me so little that I cannot even judge whether he really is encountering the problems he describes. I think he might be withholding certain information from me. Perhaps he doesn't trust me to know what he is doing or who the spies are; perhaps he suspects me of something worse than incompetence. He may already have made a full report to Suzuki, behind my back, or he may be planning to. In any case the tension between us is painfully obvious.

STUPID CRUDE AND ILLITERATE. I AM BETTER THAN THEY.

How dare they treat me this way? How dare they?

I can tell I am exhausted. I am under great strain. For the first time since my youth I have no clear idea of what the rules are, what is expected of me. I don't know what I should be doing. It is an old, familiar recipe: confusion and uncertainty mixed with fear and wounded pride. In this respect I am like a child and Suzuki's appearance here gives me the sense that correction is imminent, that punishment will follow. I resent him terribly for supporting and prolonging this—for joining the other side—by not relieving me with a word, a single word, as he could easily do at little cost to himself. I don't know why he would want to torture me but that is, in effect, what he is doing. And there are so many different words. He could say, "I am satisfied." He could say, "We will talk." He could say, "Your ignorance is no crime but it must be corrected"; he could say, "You disappoint me"; he could say nothing at all and reassign me for my failure. He could even admit his own shortcomings, his own confusion, and let us carry on as comrades. I would accept this very gladly, for he is the closest thing to my fellow in this entire continent, and I would not object to having a friend.

But none of these things even occur to him; none of these things will he do. He won't address me, he is silent, he keeps me wandering in the darkness. I am left to guess wildly at his assessment, and his intent.

And listen: I know he disapproves of Li. I know this; I'm sure it is true. Her presence can't be helping me. I have worked furiously to convince him that she is only a servant and although this is utterly impossible I think I have come close to succeeding. I think he almost believes that I would not dirty myself and my wife this way. Certainly he wants to believe it. If not for what the others tell him he might fool himself that badly, for my sake and for his own. But there is not enough basis for avoiding the truth, not even for Suzuki, and he is forced to confront it. There is too much he can't ignore.

"I see you use no other local labor," he said, as we watched her chopping vegetables at mid-afternoon.

"No," I said. "I don't have enough work for the men as it is; I don't want them to be idle."

He gestured toward her, a peculiar kind of hidden gesture as if she might see, as if he suddenly cared what she thought.

"Then let them serve you," he said. And I found I could not answer.

I cannot imagine him not thinking the worse of me for it. If I am honest, I cannot imagine him not putting his finger squarely on it and saying: here is the problem. It goes against all that he is. I have probably disappointed him most in this, more than in my performance of my duties, in point of fact; I think—I guess—that he doesn't really expect me to be a proper soldier, not really, but does desire me to be a proper Japanese. A proper, educated Japanese. He wants me to serve as a model for the men; I think he even wants to look up to me himself. And keeping her is an offense in many ways, I am gradually admitting, too many to count. It is so thoroughly *wrong*.

Oh, I can see it all, how bad it is, now that he is here. I have had such contempt for those that are with me, I have managed to heap up my scorn (of which they must be aware) until it honestly didn't matter what they thought. But the major brings me to earth; he reminds me of my shame. In his eyes I can see the eyes of all the others. I can see my family, my neighborhood, my colleagues, my friends. If I weren't me it would be nothing, if I were a farmer or a worker and a private in some outfit in Shantung or Honan I could have a hundred Chinese women—women, girls, boys, whatever—and it would simply be my "nature." No one would think the worse of me for it; dislike me, maybe, yes, even disapprove, but they would not condemn me. They would not be *disappointed*. But as the captain, as Kuroda, I have a conscience. I have free will. I am an officer who keeps a prostitute but will not allow his men the same privilege; I am a military freak who can only interfere; I am an elitist intellectual behaving in a manner he knows to be wrong. I am a good husband who betrays his good wife, a worshipped father who drags himself down. Until now I have made myself truly an exile by taking those portions of my life that I carry with me and cutting them out, pushing them away, pretending there is nothing here but China and the woman and me. But this visit puts an end to it, and beats my forehead against a wall; in Suzuki I can clearly see the censure of home.

And I don't know that I could explain it to him, even if I wanted to. I am often just as puzzled as he appears to be. Whence comes this passion for her, this bodily craving?

Where are all my former limits? What makes me feel so strongly for this one poor Chinese girl?

Affection I have had, but always of a different kind. Others have cared more than she but somehow touched me less. Admiration, yes, that too, and also respect, but what else have I been missing? What is this prize that I desire? I think of my small daughter, loving and devoted, forever hanging back until I called her to my side. I remember my wife on the night we were married—so delicate and lovely, so warm and alive, and yet so distant it seemed I could never hope to reach her. I knew to my soul that she would never have pity on me, nor see my sorrow or my pain; my heart broke then as it is breaking now, staring out at these faraway and unforgiving hills.

But Li is real as they could not be, isn't that apparent? It comes from circumstance, and from the manner of our meeting. She knew I would not harm her; for some reason she was moved. As if it mattered in the world that there were things I would not do. And then she gave to me, is what it comes down to; she gave to me and I fell in love. She rewarded me for decency and thus I was unleashed. Was I so starved and so crippled, before we ever came together? Was I so desperately in need?

Now see me trying, in my panic, to defend the indefensible. Or to explain away the blame.

Here, Major, understand: I really am a good officer. My men admire me. The garrison is secure and the population fears us and respects our power. There will be no further embarrassments. And this woman is not a whore, she is a servant, a servant—surely as commander I am entitled to some luxury. Look, she is skilled, she comes from good family. Much better than having a soldier do my chores. Actually—can I be honest with you, Major?—she is not even a servant, really. She is a charity case. Sentiment, yes; I know I am soft, I should not care. But something prompts me to do a good turn here. Something weak in my nature, perhaps noble as well. This conflict is so unfortunate and it can do no harm to try to help one innocent victim. A single young Chinese; a little trivial assistance. Will not heaven take notice? Tell me, where is the harm?

Later, about four o'clock, as we walked down toward the village—three soldiers on the road ahead and three behind—he started making hints, hints of a particular kind. He talked very freely and in a jocular vein and he seemed to be trying to convey something to me. He was glad to be at headquarters most of the time, he said, and not in the field, because the food was better. He confessed that he had picked up certain small treasures—"just one or two," he told me cheerily—from abandoned houses, and had sent them to his wife. He appreciated the privileges of rank more and more with every day, he allowed, and valued the respect that accrued to his age. He even acknowledged that he might, if he were younger, join some of the other staff with certain well-known ladies from Tokyo. However there were none of real quality, he told me, even if he were inclined to try them. There were none like the ones he had known in his youth. He almost envied the troops their weekly tickets and their comfort women, though of course these were not Japanese.

It was a warm April day with just a few clouds. The road was fairly dry and I was glad we were walking; I was enjoying the sunshine and the air and even, in a small way, his company. I was glad he was so talkative. As the village came in sight again he looked at it and sighed. "So much I miss," he said, "and so much I am missing. My duties keep me busy." He studied the village. "I wish I were here in another capacity," he said.

I felt the sun on my face and the soft breeze, and a minor sort of release, and a desire to stop and sit down on the embankment. "War," I stated carefully, "changes everything. It is hard to understand." Conscious of the soldiers' bootsteps on the road, I lowered my voice. "We are far from what we know."

He looked slyly at me. "The longer this goes on," he said, "the better we get at accommodating ourselves to it. Don't you think?"

I am trying to induce him to tell me about the war. Not my war but the one that really matters. He is so attached, from long habit, to the possession of "secrets" that he is having trouble sharing with me and even grasping how uninformed I am. How much I need to be included, at least in this way. Despite my revulsion for what we have done I do want my country to win this war. I want it badly. I want it to be over quickly, that is all; I want no one else to die.

His tongue loosened slightly as we dined in my quarters. Li had made an excellent meal and I sat there moodily hoping it would improve his opinion of her, and also mocking myself for this foolish, puerile thought. But when he began to talk, indirectly, about the campaign in the north, I became more alert. I did everything to encourage him.

"And it's all going smoothly?" I asked.

"Almost all," he said. He looked at me. "You've heard about their small success? Their little trick?"

"No. I've heard nothing. We don't get much news here."

"You've heard nothing?" He watched me closely. "Well. You are isolated."

"We seem to be," I said, "although at times I wonder why."

I didn't know whether he had missed my meaning, or was ignoring me, or honestly lacked for an answer. That is the way it is with Suzuki. "That isn't good," he said. "You should arrange to be better informed." Go ahead then, I wanted to say, suggest to me, tell me how to do that—better yet take care of it yourself, there must be units within fifty miles of us and you have only to give an order—but he leaned back in his chair.

"Hsuchow is the objective now," he said. "Another important railway junction. Another crowded, impoverished town. Of course it's just one target, there are others to the west. I can't tell you what I don't know." As I nodded he broke off and stared at me.

"No news?" he asked. "No visitors?"

"Official couriers, of course, and a few deliveries of supplies and mail—but not much information with them."

"What about the radio?"

"We get instructions and alerts and local conditions on the radio, Major," I said, "not news." Still he looked at me. "Yes, and the propaganda station, but there is little detail to it."

He grunted. "Nice word," he said. "Accurate enough."

"I don't trust it."

"You shouldn't."

"'Pacification and Soothing Corps' bulletins," I said. "Chinese puppets and the like."

He looked at me and was silent.

"I would rather hear it from you," I said at last.

He took a sip of sake. "I will see to it," he said, "that you receive reports."

I waited for him to go on. He sipped at his wine again, and smiled, and propped his elbows on the table.

"As forces came to bear on Hsuchow," he told me, "they set a clever little trap outside a small town north of there. I call it 'clever' without sarcasm; I admit that it was. It's about time they did something right. At any rate, we got in but we had trouble getting out. Losses have been high." He glanced around—Li was resting in the corner and I thought he wanted her to serve him—and then examined my face again. "I know you do not like it here but be glad you were not at Taierchuang," he said.

"On the contrary," I said. "It is to my great regret. I would be glad if some deserving comrade were well-protected here, and I in the north assuming his risk."

"Of course," said Suzuki, shifting in his chair. "No disrespect intended, Captain." Suddenly he laughed in his awful way. "I don't know about you," he went on with some vigor, "but I intend to return to my family intact. Now that we have Shanghai and Nanking—now that we've smashed their pitiful air force and can bomb the cities and railroads at will—most of the Japanese dying is over with. I think it would be silly, and not particularly honorable, to be one of the few who suffer from the poor judgment of some slow-witted general. Don't you?" He grinned at me; it excited him to talk that way. "At Shanghai, yes, you and I took risks," he said. "We both did. I remember it. At Shanghai, Japanese blood was required. Many had to die and had it been our privilege we would have died happy. But that part of the war is ended now. And I intend to live on, to properly serve the homeland."

"Perhaps," I said, "it isn't ended yet. If what you've been telling me is so."

He frowned. "A setback," he said. "An aberration. Soon they will lose the will to resist and stop fighting entirely." He breathed deeply; for a moment his lips were firmly set. "And we will take Hsuchow," he said.

Then he stood—a little unsteady on his feet, I was surprised to see, I didn't think he had drunk that much—and looked around the room. He searched until he found Li, dozing in the corner with her head on her knees, and he went to her and stood there watching her. His wine cup was in his hand, his collar unfastened. I was frightened of what he might do. A nauseating terror filled me as I realized, in a sudden rush like a wave into a rock pool, how much I had at stake. How far I was prepared to go. Before I knew it I saw myself striking him to protect her. The image enraged me and also made me want to cry.

I coughed; she woke and raised her head and saw him watching, and she stood, and waited quietly for his order. I was actually proud of her—ridiculous!—for not being frightened, at least not that I could see.

"What these people don't understand is that we are here to provide them with what they've always wanted," he said. "We are here to do them good." She was five feet away and he was looking right at her but he was talking to me, that was obvious. He knew she knew Japanese, at least a little—I had spoken to her several times that day—but he didn't seem to care. "We can give them what has always been most central to their culture," he said. "Or rather we can *restore* it, if only they will cooperate."

He looked at me but I couldn't respond. "We're not the enemy," he said, as if in argument. "The whites are the enemy." Then he turned to Li again. "The white tyrants, the white robbers," he said to her blank features. "Why won't you understand?"

He turned from her and started pacing; he went back and forth across the room. I had no idea why he was so agitated, so suddenly, why he wanted so much to convince me. His voice was very loud. However much he'd drunk there was more to it than that.

He paused to light a cigarette and began to move again. "The Japanese man sees now, sees rightly, that there must be order," he said. "There must be order in Asia. Not just in the village, not just in Japan but in Asia as a whole, among all the Five Races as in any large family. This is something the Chinese man has always understood. Perhaps the Chinese man has been too firm about placing himself at the head of the family—perhaps the Chinese man will have difficulty accepting a more equitable, a more sensible arrangement—but he has always believed in order. In order and unity. Order in each city, each province, order in the universe."

He appeared to be very much stimulated by the topic, to my surprise, not just by the wine or my company, or my relationship with Li. The strength of his passion was very plain. His smoke-trailed turns around the room became quite rapid, but I was motionless as I watched.

"And why not the Emperor?" he asked. "Why not? Theirs was not even a real Chinese, much less divine, and now they have none at all. But our Emperor is strong. Why should he not be even stronger?"

He was silent for four or five seconds as he paced and when I looked past him to the stove my eye met Li's. I was shocked—almost hurt—by her hard face, by the lack of recognition. But I believed I understood.

Suzuki stopped and turned to me. "'Citizens should obey their rulers,'" he recited. "Do you know who said that? Do you?" He waited and so did I. "It was only the great Confucius," he told me. "Confucius said that!"

I had risen by then. *What an idiotic comment.* I strove to keep my thoughts from my face.

"Should we not be Confucians in his very homeland?" he asked with great eagerness. "Should we not be Confucians in Korea and the Philippines?" He looked around at Li and then back to me again. "Yes, her too. Her too. Her and all the others here and all the Japanese, me and you and all these soldiers who've run wild. We all need family. We all need security. Everyone needs order."

What a pitiful idea.

"You are right," I said. "Who could disagree?" I gestured toward his chair. "Will you not rest now, Major, and let the servant give us more of this excellent wine that you so generously brought?"

He peered at me for a moment in the dimly lighted room—resentfully, I thought—and then sat down at his place. I spoke softly to Li and she came forward to fill our cups and clear, while Suzuki stared at the table and slowly became calm. I guessed then that it wasn't resentment I had seen but rather disappointment, or maybe sadness and fatigue.

"At any rate," he said, more quietly, "no further discussion of this country, please, or of the war. I am here on orders, yes, as part of my duties, but personally I am visiting a friend." He smiled at me, expecting something. I tried very hard to produce the words—to address him in the way in which he wished to be addressed—but I couldn't. I couldn't think of anything to say. I was afraid to open my mouth, I discovered, so I limited myself to a very solemn nod.

"Enough politics," he said. "Let us talk about science."

SIXTEEN

From the hills to the west you can see a great deal. Today the air was very clear and the valley was spread before us. We could make out every detail of the land around the schoolhouse—with his binoculars we could even see the soldiers as they worked on the bridge—and we could also see a long way east, beyond the next ridge and toward the coastal plain. It hurt my heart for a minute or two, to look that way. I don't believe I'll ever be back there. But it was beautiful to see. It was beautiful to be up high. For months now I've been living in the dirt and in caves, more or less, very close to the ground, and the broad sweep of the valley drew forth a disused part of me. I reveled, for a time, in the illusion of freedom.

The view on the other side was more remarkable still. It

seemed as if the whole of Huainan were visible, though of course that isn't possible. It was like nothing I'd ever known before. After lunch we climbed the summit behind us and as we came over the crest we were stunned by the sight of the rough, crumpled earth going on for miles and miles, brown and green, whole and structured like something living but also disjoint, chaotic, each hill and pond and field with its own character, its own presence. To the southwest I could barely see the glimmer of the Chao Hu, and the peaks of the Tapieh Shan hanging in the air. I was moved by the grandeur and so was he. Years ago I rode the train from the river toward Hofei, past the shores of the Chao and through the foothills, but I had never seen the country from above; I had never had a real idea of what it was like. Imagine living next door to such a place for so long and not knowing it! Imagine it ruined by a season of drought, or drenched and flooded by endless rain.

It is a very long time since I was out on a picnic. A picnic was something my parents liked and so we went once in a while, with food my mother packed. We took our toys and our books; we had to find a sheltered spot because if anyone recognized my father (and almost anyone would) they might present to him with symptoms, or ask for his advice, or try to take him somewhere to see a sick child. It was one of the few things we all did together. It was a most peculiar practice by local standards—I don't know where my parents picked it up—and it just added to my father's reputation. But I always had fun, and so did my brother, and I think it was a very great pleasure for my mother, who seldom left the house except to go to the market (she insisted on doing the shopping herself, though it embarrassed me) or to visit with the neighbors. She told me once that it reminded her of bringing food to her own parents in the fields, and of the delight it gave her to see their satisfaction as they ate.

When Kuroda asked me to make a meal we could take with us and then get ready to go out, fear clutched at me unexpectedly; there was an odd look in his eye and I assumed the time had finally come, that he was taking me away, taking me somewhere beyond his protection. He is trying to grow a beard—it is a patchy, bristly thing that I don't think will last—and at that moment it made him very unfamiliar, almost sinister. It added much to my uncertainty. He turned from me and as I watched his back I sought reassurance; I reminded myself of what we'd done the night before, of his tender words.

By trying very hard I fought off some of my panic, and I spoke to him calmly. "Is this an outing we're going on," I asked him, "or a journey?"

He faced me. "Just a trip into the hills," he said. "I haven't been there yet." I could see him assessing me. "What's wrong?" he asked. "Are you still so very frightened? Are you still afraid to leave here?"

"Who will go?"

"Just you and me."

"How will we go?"

"On a motorcycle."

I bit my lip and turned away and he laughed. "I'm sorry," he said. "I thought it would be nice for you. If you'd rather not I'll go by myself."

I pictured him ambushed and dead in the hills, and me left alone at the camp with the soldiers. "No, thank you," I told him, "I don't mind at all." I smiled at him, or tried to.

"I will enjoy it," I said. "I know I will. Please forgive my foolish caution. I can't help it."

His face bore such sadness then, such weight and misery, that I was strongly affected. I wondered how I could have doubted him.

The motorcycle waited at the top of the road, freshly polished by the look of it. I was very aware of the rifle on his back. He gestured to the sidecar—I know he would have helped me but there were several soldiers watching, though they all pretended not to—and I put the food on the floor and climbed in. I had never ridden a motorcycle. I watched him as he settled onto the seat and adjusted his goggles, and then started the engine. He wasn't very sure of himself and it was hard to believe he had done it before.

"Was this in your army training?" I asked him. I almost had to shout to be heard.

"No," he said loudly. "I've taken lessons from Yawata." He held the handgrips firmly and I thought we would go, but first he reached into his pocket for another pair of goggles. He gave them to me. "Put these on now," he said.

The engine was very noisy and the sensation of moving so rapidly, so close to the ground, was most disturbing. If I looked to my left I saw pebbles and dirt and green plants flying by at a high rate of speed. If I looked ahead I feared the obstacles, each stone and every patch of mud. He seemed competent enough, and I knew I had no real reason for concern—we weren't actually going very fast, it was just the newness of it that made it seem so—but it was a very unpleasant experience at first. My stomach was upset. I slowly became accustomed to it as we drove along and I relaxed just a little, but even then my hands gripped the edges of my seat so tightly that they hurt.

A few peasants in the fields turned to watch us going by. Beyond the village we passed the edge of the site on which his army had camped. There were no remaining signs of them—everything they might have left having been carried away by scavengers, I'm sure—but there were no crops planted either. The ground had a barren and damaged look, a sort of blight, as if a giant foot had descended and stamped on it again and again. I was curious about whose land it was and why no one was working it. I wondered if those who had tilled it before were all dead, or just elsewhere. It occurred to me that perhaps this was entirely within my own eyes and that the land in truth was like all the other land around it, seedlings coming up everywhere, but by then we had gone past it and I couldn't look again.

As we came to the fork and headed west I turned to the right, to try to see the schoolhouse on the top of its hill, but the motorcycle was in the way. I wished, suddenly, to be passing the grove that we had visited weeks before; I wanted to stop and look. I wanted to see the bamboo trunks with their new crowns and the *Ailanthus*, all leafed out though it was just April, the young ones sprouting green and red from the earth. Some farmer would come eventually and pull them up, I knew—to keep them from encroaching on the cultivated ground—but for a short while they would cluster around the feet of their parents, thriving. I wished we were going to the grove again, and only there; as we drove through territory I had never seen before the thought of covering so many miles, of moving so far from the safety of our chambers, made me anxious. I wanted to tell him to turn back.

Why does he take such risks? I asked myself. Amid the noise and vibration my concern for my own welfare, newly vigorous, rose up and made me angry. And why am I a part of it? Simply to allow him to feel his own power, his power over me? Is that all I'm needed for?

I looked out over the fields and thought, I know what will happen if we're attacked: they'll kill me too. And there are others, it's not just him and me. What about his family in Japan? What about the village, what monster will they send here to replace him if he dies? Probably somebody like the lieutenant. Certainly no one like Kuroda. With his help I might survive this war, which he seems to want, but how can I do that if he throws himself away? Even now the news is going out: *the Japanese dwarf is on the road, all alone*.

I turned to the rifle on my right for comfort. Did he even know how to use it? He had the rifle and his pistol, which might possibly protect us from lunatics and robbers but never from guerrillas who would snipe at us from cover. We were essentially defenseless. I thought of Nagai, left behind and in charge. Was he glad about the risk? Was that the reason he allowed it?

After half an hour or so the road curved around and began to climb steadily, moving up into the hills. I realized we were following the tracks of his army as it went north that day. In another ten minutes we reached the base of a very high hill, rising above us to our left, and he pulled the motorcycle off the road. Even there we could see some distance to the east. When he stopped the engine the silence was wonderful; I took the goggles from my face. It was another warm and sunny day—we seem to have had a lot of those this spring, though maybe I'm just noticing them more than before—and there were butterflies in the air around us, and birds calling, and the scent of many flowers. I stood and searched the roadside for a place to have our meal.

"We'll go now," he said. I looked at him. He was pointing up the hill. It was at least thirty minutes' climb to the peak, I was sure, probably more. The slope was only moderate, but steep enough to tire us going up and coming down.

"You're leaving the motorcycle here?" I asked.

He showed impatience for a moment, then quickly hid it. "I want to see the country from higher up," he said. "We can't get any higher than this on the road, not for miles at any rate. I need to climb the hill."

I dropped my goggles into the sidecar and reached down for the food. "Why didn't you come with your soldiers?" I asked.

I began to move toward him, but he approached me first and took the food from my hand. We crossed the road and started up the slope. There was a worn path that seemed to go straight to the top, with a few switchbacks here and there. He went ahead and I followed; the pace he set surprised me but I had no trouble keeping up. There were fifteen years between us, after all. I didn't like watching the gun on his back, but because I was behind I could stop without obstructing him and turn to look briefly behind us as we rose, and then walk faster to catch up.

"I explained to you," he said after a few minutes, "that I thought you would enjoy it. You live a dull and narrow life, like a prisoner." *Like a prisoner.* "I thought coming here would relieve that. I thought it would be a treat."

His voice was offhand as he spoke, very calm, but I heard what he was saying. Again I was stirred by his attachment to me. I hurried to get close to him, to touch his shoulder with my hand. He never missed a step.

"The problem," I said, "is that I'm unused to recreation. It's been so long since I did anything for pleasure that I hardly remember what it's like." He was silent and I knew I had wounded him. "And what we do together," I said. "That is for pleasure also." He wouldn't answer. "Don't be hurt," I said.

"Do not lie," he told me.

"I'm not lying," I said. "It is for pleasure. It is. But can you blame me if it sometimes seems—sometimes, not always—to be for other reasons too?"

We kept on marching up the hill and I noticed the breeze getting stronger. He didn't speak.

"It was my idea," I reminded him.

Then he stopped and turned around. "Listen," he said, "I'm well aware that you're making the best of this. Do you suppose I believe you would even consider it if you weren't so dependent on me?" His face was astonishing. He had never before revealed so much, not even in intimacy. He looked past me to the valley.

"Kuroda," I said, "I care for you."

He closed his eyes.

"I would not allow myself to be taken against my will, not more than once. I would make you kill me first."

Still he was motionless.

"I thank you," I said, "for giving me life, and your devotion. I don't know about tomorrow but right now you must believe that I think very, very well of you. I am glad of your affection and find great comfort in it."

He opened his eyes and looked at me. The wind blew

some hairs across my face and I brushed them away. I smiled at him and though he wouldn't smile back something loosened.

"You're welcome," he said.

We ate our meal on a rock overlooking the valley, warming ourselves, savoring the air and the smells and the sense of peace. We talked very little. Between bites he put his bowl down and searched with his binoculars, for what I didn't know. There was much to be discovered in the valley, I was sure, much of interest, especially to an occupying soldier. The railroad tracks lay gleaming in the sun. After a while he let me look and I enjoyed that; at one point I convinced myself, despite the mist on the horizon, that I could see the big lakes and the Grand Canal between them. But I didn't even exclaim to him, so quickly did I acknowledge it as wishful thinking. I was amused to spot the working party at the bridge—I couldn't make out the individuals, of course, but the truck and the bridge itself were easy to identify—and to watch an old man walk along the road at the foot of our hill, unaware of our presence. He gave the motorcycle a wide margin at first, but after he had passed it he started back for a moment before changing his mind again. Back and forth he went, several times, and then caution bested curiosity and he continued on his way. I pointed him out to Kuroda, who watched intently. My amusement was dampened by the thought that another Japanese, most any other, might have taken up his rifle and shot the old man down for sport.

We finished the food and put the wrappings away. As we climbed to the top to look out to the west I was overwhelmed, as I had often been before, by the strangeness of the man. By his unlikelihood, his complete inappropriateness. It seemed so ludicrous to me—his being in the army at all, his being an officer, his assignment to the garrison—and I needed to know more. I needed to know more because it had to do with my own life, my own future. If Kuroda was heaven's gift to me, what gift was for Kuroda? What had it cost him to protect me? I wanted to know his past, to hear of the odd adventures that had brought him to this extraordinary position: explaining crop rotation to a Chinese doctor's daughter on a hilltop in Anhwei. All those islands full of Japanese and how many of them were there in China with me? Only one. A single one. And the last one any sensible person might expect.

We stood and looked together at that ominous land—rugged and dusty and empty, I knew, its people driven south and west—and stole short glances at each other. Then we stopped to rest on our rock again before continuing down the slope. It was well into the afternoon and the sun was dropping; it wouldn't be very long before the hill we were on and the others around it began to block the light from the land to the east, from the schoolhouse and the village. I tried hard to find the right way to ask for what I wanted but I was nervous again, and when he edged himself closer it made me even more uneasy. I thought he was about to touch me, which I wouldn't have minded except that he had never once touched me outside of his bedroom. Never. I thought he might take me in his arms then and there. So I blurted out my question.

He didn't like it; I saw him stiffen. He said nothing, and I tried again with different words. But no response.

"I'm just puzzled," I said.

He sniffed. "Don't you Chinese like puzzles? I thought you did."

"There are four hundred million of us," I told him.

He sniffed again. "I am sorry," he said after a moment, his elbows resting on his knees. "It is something I was taught."

We sat and looked at the valley floor. I tried to be patient, and for that I was rewarded; with hesitation he explained. "A sort of promise to my father," he called it, gazing down at the river. "I didn't know if they would have me."

His story was straightforward. As I understood it, the elder Kuroda—very proud and tyrannical, from what he said, a fiercely loyal Japanese—had made him pledge, in his teens, to join the army if he were needed (this was during the big European war). He tried to describe it as a matter of honor but it sounded to me like the product of shame. Like a mistake. As he told me the tale I thought it over and marveled: this person, at the age of at least thirty-five, had actually been bullied into leaving his university and begging a commission by the scorn of an old man, by the fading promise of childhood, of another time. And not even on the basis of a threat to his country; Japan had had no need of him. It was the flimsiest example of a "war" one could imagine, a calculated foreign adventure. For no good reason, for reasons that would not have made sense to his wife or to his colleagues or his friends—possibly not even to his father!—he had agreed to travel hundreds of miles and risk his life, to become a killer and shed his scruples, at the very least to be apart from his family and his studies for years.

As he spoke to me I watched and tried to conjure up his father (an old soldier, very hard) but I couldn't, though for an instant I saw mine.

I wanted to know the rest of it, of course, the path on which he'd marched from that beginning to my barnyard, but I decided I could wait. That's enough for the moment, I told myself; you have enough to ponder now. I am a moral Chinese woman and I know about duty but this was something far beyond me, as amazing as the sky. It baffled me. Although he clearly had strong feeling he was also unselfconscious; he told me about it so casually, almost as if it bored him, as if it were the most commonplace thing in the world. He told it as if entirely unaware of the obvious conclusion: that he had not had good reason to do what he did, that some other hidden purpose must have driven him onward.

"I hope your father is proud of you," I said.

"I'm sure he's dead by now."

"Excuse me?"

"I'm sure he's dead."

I was astonished by the way he said it. So lightly but with confidence.

"You don't actually know?"

"Last I heard he was terribly sick. He was very sick even when I left Japan. I haven't had a letter from home in almost four months and I think he has probably died. If not he will soon."

"I see," I said quietly. "If you do get word, will you go home to show respect?"

He stretched his arms out to either side of him, palms open, to take in the valley and the river and the ridge and all the land beyond it, beyond it to the sea. "Tell me, please, how do I leave here?" he asked me. "Supposing I wanted to, how do I go?"

Soon after that he got up and started walking but I stayed

where I was and called to him. I patted the rock and made him sit down again, right beside me, and then I leaned against him. His arm went gently around my waist and I put my head on his shoulder. It was a very unusual feeling but also familiar. I might have been, once again, on a picnic with my parents. I was no longer afraid that he would want me on the spot; I took our contact then as friendship and no more, and I believed he felt the same. Gradually it came to me that I was finally relaxed after a whole day of worrying. I wished it hadn't taken me so long to get to it. It was very soothing. I wanted to stay there, to stay until morning, though I knew we needed plenty of time to climb down and drive back to the schoolhouse before dusk.

But then he began to recite something. It was verse of some kind and didn't sound Japanese. He said it slowly and I tried to listen carefully but I couldn't really follow it, maybe because I didn't know some of the words he was using. It just distressed me as I listened. It was about death, it seemed, about death and love, and it frightened me to hear him. His arm was still around me; I know he felt me drawing away but he kept on and did not turn. When he finished he released me.

"What is it?" I asked, after a few silent seconds.

"A poem," he said, "by an Irishman. A poet named Yeats."

Why would a man like you know such a thing?

He sighed and got to his feet. "I translated it myself when I was in school," he said. "I was very romantic then, almost mystical, at least compared to now. Very foolish. When I first saw the poem, in English, I was fascinated. I knew it was profound. I thought if I could really understand it I might understand the world. I wanted to broaden my mind beyond Japan." He smiled slightly and very briefly and started brushing off his pants. "So I studied until I could translate it properly, and I've remembered it since."

He thinks I understood it.

"Speaking of dying," I said out of nowhere, the words coming quickly, "you do know that it's insane for us to be out here like this, don't you? Absolutely insane?"

He looked at me steadily, almost smiling again but not quite. I was frustrated by his silence.

"The communists. The bandits. Even the regular army," I said. "Nothing would make them happier than to kill you." I waited for his answer but there was none. "And if they kill you," I went on, "they'll kill me also, as a traitor. Another reason for concern."

He stood there looking down at me. It was a very long time, or so it seemed. "I apologize," he said. "I apologize for my ignorance. As I said before, I thought it would be nice for you. I am sorry it was difficult instead."

"It was nice," I said. "It was very nice. But I'm frightened, I can't help it."

He held out his hand (no glove this time) and pulled me to my feet. I realized that my legs were tired. He turned around and crouched to pick up his rifle and his binoculars and the knapsack, then turned again to face the east.

"I understand," he said softly. "I'm frightened too. It's just bravado." We looked over our shoulders to the summit at our backs. The sun was about to fall behind it. "We won't ever do it again," he said. "I promise. Now shall we go?"

SEVENTEEN

There is a silence that comes slowly to this camp, late at night. More and more I seek it out. I entertain it and it entertains me; we comfort each other; it restrains me, inhibits me, keeps me from crying in the darkness. I welcome it. It is a silence so impersonal and so meticulously fair that it helps me to forget not only my own troubles but also the troubles of those around me: my servant, my men, the townspeople, the many restless dead. It comes to shelter and transfigure us. When I sit here with my candle in this ocean of quiet I can almost believe that we are other than what we must be, what we have steadily become. I can almost believe—almost—in a chance to start again.

I don't know why I told her. I should not have. I don't know why. I meant only to enjoy a little outing, a silly attempt to relieve the dreary days in which we live, but now I have added *disloyal* to my sins. As if I had not already done enough that was wrong. If my father is dead I'm sure he knows what I told her; if he isn't I must live with the fear that he'll find out. Either way it grieves me. I know it is as nothing compared to my involvement with the enemy, my lack of enthusiasm for the war—my *treachery*, as he would call it—but those are political and this is personal, and crossing that boundary seems particularly bad. To me, if not to him. He may adore the Emperor, he may consider being Japanese more important than being my father, but I can't free myself from him; I know of nothing more important than the fact that I'm his son.

Two years ago, before they sent me overseas, I was stationed for a month in Tokyo. I was passing by the Palace on assignment one day and saw a fruit sitting on the ground, just outside the wall. It had fallen from an overhanging bough. Without taking even a moment to think I quickly retrieved it, a very risky thing to do, and hid it safely in my pocket. Later on I boxed it up and sent it to him, with a note explaining. It was all impulse. As soon as I mailed it I regretted it, I decided he would be furious, but I was wrong; it turned out, my mother wrote, that he was fully overcome. It was the kindest thing I had done for him since childhood, perhaps the kindest ever. When I saw him next his eyes were gleaming, and he actually took my hand.

I was not prepared for her to ask me. I did not expect it—because I was looking at the landscape and distracted by her smell, because we had already embarrassed each other once that afternoon, because she had never shown an interest—but beyond that I was not prepared. It is a question I have been unable to ask myself, much as I've wanted to, for months, for years, in fact for all my life, and out of this inability has come a willful ignorance. I have learned to pretend that the question does not exist, could not exist, and as a result I no longer have defenses against it; that would not be playing the game. So she caught me answerless. It was like hearing something awful for the first time, when she spoke to me, like a doctor calling my office to say my daughter was burned in a fire.

"Kuroda, what are you *doing* here?" she asked.

I looked out over the valley.

More softly: "How did you come to be an officer?"

It was difficult not to be angry at first; her tone was so incredulous. I'm sure I answered with something bitter. I wanted to strike her, to leave her, to ask her in turn: How did you come to be an orphan? How did you come to be a prisoner? What makes you think you are the only one who is victimized, compelled, the only one who suffers by a circumstance of birth?

But then I took a breath and found a gentler perspective: she was curious after all. She did want to hear about my own small tragedy, my own misfortune—that was why she asked. It was progress of a sort. I recalled the occasions on which I had tried, timidly, to tell her more about myself, to reveal or explain, before giving it up in the face of her indifference. Now she wanted to be told and I would have to do my best.

She listened carefully. She was very attentive. It was almost as if I were back in my classroom. Despite my unreadiness—despite my desire to keep my painful feelings hidden—I was gratified that she wanted to know. And it did me good to organize my thoughts; it was an echo of the rigor with which I used to live my life. In this place I am the farthest thing from organized. Here instead of rigor I have the ennui of an exile, all mixed up with giddiness and torment over Li. Instead of study and well-planned lectures I have hour after aimless hour, instead of a schedule of appointments I have the agony of a day to be gotten through without making mistakes—without blundering in front of the men, without putting her at risk, without doing something else I'll have cause to regret if I ever survive this "incident" and return to my orderly life and my books.

Before long I saw the clouds of disapproval on her face, or at the least of disbelief, but once started I couldn't stop or even slightly change my course; she had asked and she would hear it. If it made her think poorly of me perhaps that is appropriate. If she means to go on sleeping with a Japanese captain then she had better understand.

And I confess that I resent her disapproval. I resent it. There is much she does not see. So what if I am here because I promised my father? So what if my presence is misguided, a waste, or even worse does active harm? I tried to make it clear to her that one thing followed another, the way the sapling follows the seed. That I was blinded at the time. I tried to give her to understand that you cannot stop a man's life at a certain point *so* and state its meaning then and there, judging it as you would a painting or a house or the blueprint for a ship, something planned and executed with conscious design. Remember this, I wanted to say: he is my *father*. He is my life, literally my life; I would not have it but for him. You speak Japanese because your father did, because his father chose to marry a woman of Japan, and as a result you are not dead. You are safe here with me. But the weakling you married was also chosen by your father, I'm sure he was, and had you married someone else you might not have been deserted, you might not have been abandoned to the monsters of war. You might not have needed me at all. My father did for me just what your father did for you: he cursed and blessed me all at once. That is what a father is for. One day my daughter will say the same.

I know you, I wanted to say. Believe me, I know too well the anger that you hold.

I suppose I should thank her for not asking more questions. I suppose I should be glad that she accepted what I said, without derision—despite the message in her eyes—to end an awkward situation. But it wasn't courtesy, not entirely. It was that, but also that she's smug. She thinks she understands me but she doesn't; she thinks I was telling her a tale of pure woe but that is far from the truth. It sickens me to be so open to this woman and yet be hiding from her, hiding as I always have (although I'm hiding different things). She actually sees my kindness, even my passion, and that is almost a miracle; she knows me as no woman has and I am very grateful for it. But we have not made full disclosure. No more than I allow myself to speak of literature to Private Sugimura can I reveal to her that I am entirely Japanese in any number of ways, that I am truly my father's son.

I did as he told me then, yes, did it willingly; I do as the army tells me now. I am loyal, I am obedient, I am diligent up to a point. As difficult as it is becoming I still strive to believe in the Emperor, Li, in the Path and the Will of Heaven. Sometimes my skin crawls to think that I am surrounded by so many Chinese—Chinese peasants, common coolies. And it is more than duty, more than training that moves me;

it is enrichment, fulfillment, the eager pursuit of that for which I was formed.

Yes, it made me happy to do my father's bidding. Yes, it pleased me to satisfy him. Of course it was humiliating when he begged me a commission—begged it from his military "friends" who are not fit to serve as his dustbin—but it was also intensely pleasurable, most gratifying, as finding an itch long unscratched. And I took quickly to the regimented life. I embraced it as my own. I refused to reveal even to my wife how much it suited me to be told where to stand, when to sleep, even how I should speak to my fellow human beings, depending on the emblems on their arms.

But the most horrible secret of all is that before the nightmare, before Nanking, before they made me a captain and cursed me with responsibility, *I liked being brave*; *I liked killing Chinese*. I was almost to the point of being grateful to my father for having sent me to Manchuria. In the midst of my disgust at taking part in such an enterprise was a private, budding pride in my success as a warrior. A success, Li. A certified China-murderer. The day I charged that trench outside Shanghai was the best day of my life, in a way, its highest point; it was certainly the day on which I was most nearly free. It is true that it led to recognition and promotion, and the end of my chances of sliding through the war unnoticed. But it was worth it. It was almost worth it. It was almost worth the blood of all the men I killed, and the weeping of their families. As the pinnacle it was also the beginning of my descent, yes, my descent to pits of loathing, but from its vantage I could see far in both directions—forward and back, ahead and behind, as the two of us did from the hilltop today—and I learned much of what I am.

The image of my father on a mat or in his grave (and of green-clad figures falling, falling stiffly as I shot them) brought death very close, and soon made me go silent. I wondered if it wouldn't be best to end both her life and my own, right then and there, with my gun or by leaping from a cliff. I thought it would deprive us of misery only, nothing more. I wanted badly to leave the hill then but she chose that moment to show me a kind of affection she had never shown before; I guessed that she felt sorry for me. Of course I could not resist.

She was relaxed, as we sat there—she almost went to sleep on my shoulder—and I was hopeless and melancholy. I should not have been surprised when the poem came back to me, so completely after so many years, but I was, at least a little. I was until I saw how closely it resembled the way my heart was hurting me, how much it helped me to bear the pain of watching Li and my father combining slowly within me, in some obscure place, a place I contained but could not reach, could find but not identify.

I wished fiercely that I could say it in Chinese. I had never had that wish but I had it then. Failing Chinese I wished I could say it in English—really say it without sounding like a fool—and that she could understand. Japanese seemed a poor substitute. I wished I was reciting it at sunset; I wished I was reciting it in Kiangsu, in her parents' visiting room; I wished I was reciting it in a barren field by the Irish Sea with the stars coming out, and the lamps of a village shining at us from the slope.

> Were you but lying cold and dead,
> And lights were paling out of the West,

You would come hither, and bend your head,
And I would lay my head on your breast;
And you would murmur tender words,
Forgiving me, because you were dead:
Nor would you rise and hasten away,
Though you have the will of the wild birds,
But know your hair was bound and wound
About the stars and moon and sun:
O would, beloved, that you lay
Under the dock-leaves in the ground,
While lights were paling one by one.

I felt stupid as I finished. I felt almost nonsensical. Why did I ever need to know such a thing? When exactly was it that I chose to be insane? But still—"He Wishes His Beloved Were Dead." Yes, that's it. I am not at all surprised that it came to me then. And I hope she understands.

I would like to be glad now, waiting here in the silence, that I unburdened myself to her. I would like to believe that she really knows me better. But though she seemed to gain a little, to appreciate my position—to appreciate what I told her, at any rate, if not what I left out—in the end I was frustrated, I was defeated. By my own omissions, yes, by my own limitations, but defeated nonetheless. In the end it came to nothing but wasted air. If I answered her at all I should have kept it very simple; I should not have tried to do what cannot be done, to create a fragile bridge across a gorge that is too wide. Love, even love, cannot prevent the bridge from falling.

My father was a soldier. He commanded on his deathbed. That is what I should have told her; that would have been sufficient. At some times the plainest of truths is enough.

WATER

EIGHTEEN

I go more often to the village now. I'm less frightened than I was and always have a soldier with me. He chooses my escorts carefully, I assume; I don't doubt that there are many who would shoot or rape and stab me and tell a tale of bandit ambush, but so far I have never been mistreated. Usually I go with Yawata but sometimes with another. They all seem so young. They tend to hurry me, of course—they're eager to get back to the protection of their fellows—and I don't blame them. I'd hurry too. To me it is all the same; I have concern about my safety wherever I am, even in Kuroda's bed, but I have grown accustomed to it. It is my typical condition.

I go to the village very often now but the more I go the more they mistrust me. The market women look at me, they attack me with their eyes. Many refuse to speak at all and we do our business in silence. My sisters? I don't know them. I don't know them and they don't want to know me. They tell themselves— they fantasize—that I am no part of them, that I am alien altogether, as if no decent Chinese woman could be where I am, as if everything I've been through is according to my preference and I have chosen to discard them and become one of the enemy.

In a way it is very like my childhood and my youth, before I went to the city with my husband. Beneath the recent devastation there is much that has not changed. The basic outlines are familiar: the same lack of empathy, the same willful misunderstanding, the same readiness to condemn that which is different. It goes from there. In both the village and the town no one asks what happened to you; they are interested only in what you have become. If that legless beggar in the street was maimed protecting his neighbor's children, it is of no concern to them. They care that he is a cripple, nothing more. He is precisely equivalent to the drunkard on the next corner, ruined by venereal disease, or to the half-Caucasian son of a Hangchow bar girl on the next. They all have flaws, visible flaws, flaws that render them unacceptable, and the truth is that it doesn't take much to make a flaw; the range of human failings that will do is very broad.

You might think that the war would have altered all of this, but you would be wrong. You might think that under the weight of invasion greater allowances would be made, but then you would be missing the point. It is not that there is ever a good reason for being freakish; the question that really matters is, how freakish are you? And just as important—how well do you hide it? How well do you blend with the masses around you? I was never any good at hiding, never able to make myself into the fully acceptable woman or girl that my mother, my husband, even my father wanted me to be; to start yearning for it now would be the height of absurdity. I suppose I might have managed it at last, this past winter, by being one of the dead—by giving in—but I made a decision not to and by now it's much too late. It isn't possible anymore. Today is just the same as those days long ago; I am doing what I must to survive, as I did in earlier years, and now as then I'm hated for it. But so be it. I accept it. I am getting far too old for any basic change in life.

And whose fault would it be, really? Is it them or is it me? Every day they eat the bitter and if you eat bitter, you become bitter; that much is very plain. But what excuse have I?

The fact is that if I'm fair, if I'm honest, I can understand their attitude toward me. The fact is that I look well, not a bit like a suffering prisoner, and I am better off than they. It would be natural enough to assume that I have come to an understanding, that I am a willing collaborator, and the beast soldiers are so hideous and have done such terrible things that it would then be very easy to despise me for it, and to consider me a traitor. Deep down I'm rather worried that even if I do outlast the occupation I'll be marked for punishment by my own people. The thought that they might hurt me now—while I'm consorting with the enemy—is not so troubling. As I say, I'm accustomed to it, and just as I won't blame myself for my misfortunes I'm prepared to accept any logical consequence, to endure the next arbitrary event, whatever it might be. But the idea that I might actually get through this, might come out the other side, and never make it to a new life in Shantung or Hupeh because some commissar or tax collector has my name on a list—that is hard.

That dismays me. It almost makes me want to cry. I wish I could at least try to address it, to gain some sympathy, by telling my side of the story—by finding someone in the village who would listen for a minute—but this is very unlikely. No one will have that kind of conversation with me; beyond their deep suspicion they keep their distance from my soldiers. It is as if we have no connection whatever, as if I do not speak their language. As if I'm held fast in a trap.

Through it all I stay hopeful. There is a part of me that searches for one caring face, one tiny smile, a single glance that shows how it appreciates my position. I don't find them—I rarely find them—but I look, I always look. It makes it easier to bear.

Of course I could be mistaken. Maybe they don't really hate me. Maybe they're just frightened. The market ladies, anyway; they're women too, as helpless as I, and they have all been in my place. Some do hate me, I'm quite certain, but a few must understand. At least a few. Maybe part of what I see is their concern for me, their worry, all mixed up with peasant caution; they could easily believe that if they speak or show a sign they'll do me harm. Silence is rarely a burden to the poor, and most often it's a friend.

Whatever the case they reveal very little, so my errands are largely uneventful. It is only in our eyes and in our postures, for the most part, in the gestures of our hands, that one can see what is between us. Most of the time it goes in this quiet way. But on occasion it erupts into something more substantial; a few of the villagers who clearly are against me, particularly certain older ones, cannot contain themselves. Even with Yawata standing by they speak their minds.

One afternoon not long ago, the egg woman—who up

until then had been most proper, expressionless and close to silent—was suddenly transformed by her loathing for me. Her face became vivid with rage and the cords tightened in her neck. She beat the top of the crate before her with the flat of her hand, heedless of her inventory. She dared to hiss her angry words.

"Your Japanese devils—they burned half of Shansi! A thousand villages or more, you can smell it from here! They roasted children in their beds!"

"They're not mine," I said politely, "and I wish they were in hell. Now may I please have seven eggs?"

So she handed them over.

For all its differences this place is very like Kiangsu. It is much like what I've known. To be in the market and the village brings memories, not only of childhood but of my later return to my parents' home, to their country town. My return to endless shame. Then as now I was a misfit to begin with, unable or unwilling (I'll be honest) to get along; then as now they had more reason to condemn me. It is true that I didn't go about with an armed guard but in a sense I might as well have, for I was the doctor's daughter and they could not afford to offend me, or to offend me very much. Even the officials' daughters and the landlords' daughters could not afford it. Everyone gets sick sooner or later. Not that my father would have taken any notice—he was too decent to withhold his services from anyone, though I suppose if he were here he wouldn't treat the Japanese—but they were really very careful. And they were usually polite. It was almost as good as a thug with a rifle.

The only real difference between that exile and this is that then I had my family. Then I had my mother and father to care for me. I had my brother to make me laugh, when he visited from Tsingtao. I had the familiar furnishings of our home, my beloved feather bed, good food that I didn't have to cook for myself. They were companions, my family, they were my allies, they were concerned; when I wept they stayed by me until I stopped. Until I felt better. Now I have no one, and when I weep—desperately, wildly, at the thought of what is lost—I take great care to do it alone and in silence. I do not want him to think he can become what they were. It is impossible by his nature.

At night I sometimes wonder about my brother, who smiled so often. Where is he? What happened to him? I even wonder about my husband. Both of them dead—it could easily be so. They could be dead or they could be in one army or another, or a guerrilla band, or maybe marking time like me. I'll never find out but it gives me something to do, this speculation. It fills my mind. In any case I don't expect to see them again.

At least I know where my parents are. That pleases me. I think if I went back there—I know I won't want to, I'm sure I won't be able to, but if I did—I could even find the place. I made no marker but I stood there for a long time, studying the landscape, trying to distinguish what would endure from what would not. A wind had come up and I had to keep my eyes half-closed against the flying ash, but I noted each detail. It was all I could do. I couldn't help or comfort them but at least I made sure of their undisturbed rest. At least I know they are safe, beyond any ill will. No one can bayonet my father now; no one can violate my mother. They are out of harm's way.

And in Anhwei, seven duck eggs. A turnip. A pint of

cooking oil. I held the same things in my hands at high noon, in a basket, in the market with my mother. With the bright sun streaming down. The same eggs, the same people, the same town years ago. The same town that didn't want me. It is all of it the same.

But how can I blame these country people? How can I blame them for even a second? Of course they think badly of me. Of course they are angry. How can I be so arrogant, so smug as to resent them, how can I possibly ascribe it to their class or to their ignorance, of all things, to provincialism, as if being the mistress of a Japanese captain were like coming home from Shanghai in a fashionable hat? Imagine if I had relatives here, had found someone to protect me, if I were selling duck eggs in the market instead of her. Then I would hate me too! I would be on the other side.

I could see myself then, anyway; I could see my own face. It's peculiar to say it but I'm not Li anymore, I don't think. I stopped being her some time ago and I'm not even sure I could recognize her now because I don't know what she looks like. I wish I could watch her from wherever I wanted; I wish I could study her. I wish I could look at her, directly at her, and truly see.

If I was a misfit or a hermit I always knew who I was, in Kiangsu and Shanghai. If they accepted or rejected me I knew who I must be. But now the very idea is a joke, a mockery, as far beyond me as the moon. I have no *essence*, no *substance*. I have no *affiliation*. When I am with him I am one thing, when I am with them I'm another. And when alone I am not anything. If I were standing in the sunshine with my mother again I would melt down, like wax, I would melt into a pool at her feet. They could take me and make of me whatever they wanted. When the egg woman looks at me I don't know who she's seeing, so help me I don't, and it binds me up with terror.

It's as if I'm in a maze or in a hall of polished brass, some kind of vain amusement gone dreadfully wrong. I try to find the exit, I try to find myself, but I can't. They won't permit it. I turn back; I spin around. At intervals I think I am escaping from confusion—I think I almost see me as I am, or as I should be, half-revealed— but then I'm lost again, suddenly. I'm lost in space and wandering. What has happened? What has happened? How in heaven was I captured by this labyrinth I'm in?

"Take care," said one thin woman as she counted up my pennies. A sadness moved across her face.

I stared back in astonishment. "Excuse me?" I said.

"Take care," she said again. "Take care of yourself." I turned around to look but there was no one there behind me. She had fixed me with her eye.

"I'll try," I managed to say.

To think that I have come to this. To think that I have fallen so low. I am wholly without virtue; I have lost my good sense, my perspective, my morality, my pride. This man is simply using me four times a week and I regard it as a kindness. A *kindness*. What degradation I've embraced; how weak and fearful I've become!

I cannot give in. I mustn't give in. I hate the Japanese—I *hate* these stinking, shuffling dwarves—and I hate their horrible crimes. Nothing can change that, nothing. They disgust me, I abhor them to the center of my being. I do. I hate them all. I hate them and I hate their lackeys. I hate their puppets, I hate their whores, I hate myself. Yes. Yes, I do.

NINETEEN

My soldiers despise me. I understand this. I have made a mess of everything. If I satisfy them now that is only as it should be, an overdue correction of my weak and blundering ways. If I fail them it simply reaffirms their condemnation. I think if I were more like what they want me to be, more properly authoritarian, more Japanese—more the modern samurai in my behavior toward them—they would forgive me the rest of it. It is strength that they respect and were I strong they would be loyal. But I am not strong, not in their terms, and so they judge me on my choices. In this sense also I am wanting.

I find it strange that I have no desire to judge them in return. That I will not protect myself by remembering who they are: ignorant, bigoted dullards before the war began, willing murderers and rapists—cheerful followers of the order, *kill this nation*—while it goes on. Some of them were criminals before they ever saw China, released from prison to join the army. (I know this is true, I heard about it from a sergeant.) They are really nothing but a mob. The propagandists tell them they are heroes, that our actions are "defensive," that this country is "anti-Japanese," that the "Co-Prosperity Sphere" is going to save us from the whites, but this is just a pointless game. The men don't care and they never have. They hate the Chinese, yes, but I don't think they even know that it is Chinese they are killing. They would kill anyone. They would go where they were told. In Nanking they made horrors they could never have imagined, made them easily and gladly, because it pleased their superiors. Because the others did the same. Because they were there.

But none of this seems to matter to me. I cling to them—I continue to allow them to punish me with their disapproval—because I depend on their sanity. I depend on it for mine. I am from Japan, I was born there, my past is there (there, where my wife and child are waiting) and I will return to Japan one way or another, live or die. I can never escape it. And the soldiers are my fundament; how could I exist without loving them? How else could I endure my ceaseless questions and my doubts? I have given up my honor but I still have my nature. I still have Kuroda. In the end, self has nothing to do with wisdom, with intelligence, with righteousness; there is not a thing about me that makes me better than they. They are my brothers.

"If a great man were to establish laws, justice could not fail to flourish," said Jimmu Tenno, and he did and it did not, but still he made us Japanese. We have no justice, no peace, but we are a people. A Japanese people. I simply cannot let that go.

I suppose if I were to murder Li that would mollify them. That would probably be enough to regain their full allegiance. If I were to execute her myself, right in front of them, and leave her body lying there. Then they would think well of me. I would again have their respect.

Or I could kill myself instead—the only honorable thing. I think I might except for Li.

Can I do what I am doing and remain Japanese? Would my ancestors be outraged or would they see it as just? *This is what you do with a woman*. Especially one with no home and no family. Make use of her; avail yourself. Take pleasure where you find it. After all, you are risking your life. The reports once again speak of fighting nearby; you may be killed in battle tomorrow, next week, next month. You are a soldier and a conqueror, you've made yourself one. She is rightfully yours.

The things we can imagine—it has always astonished me. The things we can imagine and the lies we're forced to say.

I am weeping at this moment, although I didn't think I could. I am so very alone now. Suzuki is dead. It is a terrible occasion and my entire soul is hollow. I did not know how much it would hurt me to lose him. I would laugh at the idea were it not for my grief. It is a grief I can taste, a grief that wraps itself in me; it cannot be what it seems to be, it cannot be the worst that could have happened, but it is very, very bad. To my surprise it changes everything.

A corporal came before sunset with the news. I am mystified—why this sudden need to inform me?—but it doesn't matter. Perhaps Suzuki left instructions. The corporal seemed to know why he was there, at any rate, and he studied me carefully as he handed me the message. He might have been present when my friend was killed. He might have seen it with his own eyes. I wanted to ask him but something prevented me. He certainly seemed to expect my questions; he waited patiently for a long time as I read and reread the two dozen words, as I stared out the window, wondering if I would ever meet my new commander.

But I was stubborn; something prevented me. I thanked him and praised his courage, and said I would be pleased if he would eat and rest with my men before starting back the next day. Then I told him he could go.

He was killed in an attack. That much was in the message. An attack on another garrison—on another, not mine. I don't know if I'm glad of that. It could just as well have been here. They gave me very little detail, nothing to help me imagine the scene. Only the news that he was dead, that partisans had killed him, that I would now be responsible to a Colonel Makashima in Kiangsu, that he would arrange for an inspection "at nearest opportunity." The message was not even signed. Somehow that enrages me. It is so remorseless, this rejection of our manhood. It is so thorough and complete. Poor Suzuki, shot or stabbed or blown up outside a railway station or in a farmhouse or running across a field, lying amidst the shouting and the gunfire and concussion and the screams, calling for his wife, wishing with the last contractions of his heart that he had stayed at headquarters, taken another assignment, been rotated back to Manchuria or even home to Japan. Poor Suzuki. I wonder if he thought of me. I wonder if he had time.

I see him there before my eyes, in white and red. I see him in all his purity, his sincerity. Like any good dead Emperor's soldier.

There is a limit, I've discovered. There is a limit to my tolerance. Surrender is weakness, and weakness is surrender. Apparently even I can be maddened; even I can be brought to the point of blind emotion. Even I can abandon any sense of truth or fairness and turn my anger on the latest random agent of misfortune. I robbed myself of what I most cared for, I admit that, and my countrymen took the rest, but now these people have cut the last thread. They have undone that silly, shallow, self-important man, a man who wanted only to get home safe and sound. A man who wanted to win the war so that everyone could benefit. He was a fool but he meant them no harm. He did harm but he did not mean it. He did harm to them and now they have harmed him but he was mine and they are not. I curse them. They have taken what was mine.

CHINESE DIE. CHINESE DIE. CHINESE DIE.

What a picture I make. Resting here in this chair, holding tightly to the message, wanting to do anything—smoke cigarettes, drink wine, exercise, run myself through—that would help me move beyond this, able to do nothing but sit quietly in the darkness. With Li waiting in the next room, watching over our dinner. She knows something is wrong. She knows I am unhappy. But she will wait out there without disturbing me, forever if necessary, stirring the pot, stoking the stove, sweeping the floor and scrubbing the walls. It isn't that she fears me, I don't think, or is afraid to hear my news—although of course she is imagining any number of wild things—or that she doesn't care for my feelings. It is just the way she is. She was that way at six, I'm quite certain, and she was that way with her husband. It has nothing to do with the war, or with me. It is her essence to wait.

I would like to be able to discuss it with her. Who else? I would like to call her in to hear me grieve. I don't know if I can. I will continue to adore her, to possess her, to ease myself in her as long as I am able, but I don't know if our closeness extends itself to this. I doubt that our strange joining allows us to be all of what we are at any time, even for the briefest moment; when I go to her and she comes to me we leave parts of us behind, we divide ourselves, so that I am not oil to her water, or she water to my oil, but rather something in between.

I suppose the score is even now—we killed her parents and they killed my Suzuki—but I don't think that will help. I don't think it will allow us to be whole. In fact, I'm sure it won't; it just deepens the conflict, the paradox, the frustration of our intimacy, perhaps to the point of destroying it. It is certainly much better not to tell her at all. I believe I can manage that. I have asked too many questions and have found out far too much, and I will spare her that same burden.

If she asks I will not answer. She really doesn't need to know.

TWENTY

I wonder sometimes about the rest of the country. They can't have taken all of it. It's much too big and there are too many of us, far too many to keep track of. And there aren't enough of them.

The southern and western provinces are probably untouched. Where else could the people who lived here have gone? Chances are they headed west; I'll bet Szechwan is getting full. The Japanese can't have marched all that way. Or this garrison wouldn't be where it is. On the railway or in a town, yes, but never out here in this valley. We must be at the front or near it.

West and south of me, then, there are places I could go. Huge Chinese provinces, relatively whole. And I'm sure there are scattered free territories too—even back behind the lines. Free territories and guerrilla kingdoms. They can't be hard to find. If I ran now I might reach one, or I might escape to Hankow or Changsha.

Because I have to ask myself—what happens from here? This war could last forever. It could last for years, but I won't. I can't. He'll be killed or I'll be killed or something will happen to ruin our relationship. To make it impossible. Something will come between us. Our feelings for each other—or I should say, his feelings and my actions, since I sleep with him so gladly although I do not share his passion—are so absurd, so unreal, so incomprehensible to me that I can't begin to predict what would upset them. Perhaps he'll kill some villagers; perhaps he'll burn the whole place down. Perhaps he'll decide he can no longer afford the contempt of his men. (They know by now I'm not just chattel, everyone sees his attachment to me.) Or he might grow tired of me, eventually, or too ashamed of himself to continue. The sort of thing that happens all the time.

But these grim speculations are beside the point, I know; there is too much that could go wrong, even if he and I were to continue undisturbed, too much that threatens our peace. The soldiers on the one side and the villagers on the other are like a pair of giant ocean waves, waiting to smash down on my head and drown me. To sweep me away. Battles and bombings and partisans aside, if I stay near these people long enough they'll find a way to get me; they'll find the means. There are dozens of them, hundreds, and I'm alone. I have only him.

Is this a burden I've created? Not just now, but all my life? Do I enjoy enduring solitude, playing the outcast, being hated and misunderstood? I am forced to suspect it. I'm only doing what I must, it's true, but I am wise enough to know that there is never just one way. Something about this situation appeals to me, I think. As alarming as that is. It gives me pain and little pleasure but there's a woman within me who finds it both fitting and just.

It isn't only the war. It isn't only the danger. Even if the invasion were to end this afternoon I'd have no future—no more than I had before he found me, and considerably less than I had a year ago. I was doing badly then but at least I had assistance. I entertained moments of hope. Today, nothing. What are the possibilities? What could happen? I couldn't go with Kuroda; I wouldn't want to if I could. And I couldn't stay here, they might kill me. I couldn't go back to Kiangsu. I could start off in some random direction and try to gain a fresh identity, I suppose, make a completely new life, but it was risky for a woman to travel on her own even before the Japanese came. I don't think I could bear to take up with some man for the sake of protection. Not after all of this. And I have no real skills, nothing that stands by itself; without nice clothes and spending money and the right introductions I'd never get any job worth having, anything other than the meanest factory labor. Which would put me at my neighbors' mercy again.

But now. Right now, this instant. If I ran right now—when there are so few peasants left and they stay in at night, when he would make sure no one chased me, when people are afraid to cause trouble and attract the Japanese—I might manage to reach somewhere worth reaching. I covered ground before and I can do it again; two or three weeks of travel, with some food in a sack and a waxing moon, and I could go at least two hundred miles—enough to take me to southern Honan, eastern Hupeh, even Kiangsi. (Though I know nothing at all about getting through the mountains. That would surely make it harder.) I remember talk of a Red base in southwestern Anhwei, on the border, a sympathetic area, and there must be something left of it. It could even be bigger. Maybe I could get to them, or they might find me.

The point is, if I can join up with those people who exploded the bridge, or the government if there is one, or even missionaries somewhere—if I can find someone to accept my labor and give me rice and a piece of the floor in return—I can tell them whatever I like. They will welcome me as the victim of any horror I care to describe; my word will never be doubted again. I can create any past I want to have, any history, and it will instantly be real.

All of this—a new start, a new me, even a new name, freedom from fear of the troops and the townspeople, a chance to help win the war—in return for a small risk. The risk of death or terrible suffering, yes, and maybe not small, maybe large, but have I anything to lose? Is it worse than staying here? I don't think so. I'm sure not. Short of taking his revolver and putting a bullet in my head (something I've considered many times, many times) I can't conceive of any plan that makes more sense. If good luck comes my way I am rescued and free, if it doesn't the end won't last too long. I would never run off with his gun but I could certainly take a knife and have it ready, to draw across my throat. Who knows, I might even be able to defend myself. I'd be willing to try.

If I were truly very brave I'd take one of their horses. I don't know that it's possible but it would be worth some thought. On a horse I could travel very quickly, very far, and

I love the picture it makes for me—timid Li riding bareback through the night. But then he would have to send someone after. Otherwise not. If I took something large he'd have to try to get it back, but if he possibly could he'd let me go.

I'm so very convincing. I almost put myself to flight. It's too bad I don't have an audience, that I can't give a lecture on What She Should Do because I'm sure there'd be applause. I see no flaw in my argument; I've even memorized a list of things to take with me. And I've guessed—I think I'm slowly coming to believe—that it's just what he expects.

So I should go. Why don't I go? I have no idea, none at all. It isn't fear. It isn't logic. There is no reason in heaven or on earth why I don't but I don't. I'm not ready to, that's obvious, the only obvious thing. Willing I am, even prepared, but not ready. I don't know why.

I want to be more like *Ailanthus*, I suppose, not less. That could be part of it. I don't want to run, to be blown across the landscape, to be fragile and to hide. I have never really had any presence to speak of but now I want to be like the tree of heaven. I want to have a place. It puts down such deep roots, that tree, such strong ones; it puts down its roots to survive. Of course when someone comes for it, to pull it up or burn it, it has no way to escape—it is fixed to its position—but this hardly matters because there are always others. Always another specimen somewhere. One sapling may be taken, a hundred shoots, ten thousand trees, but *Ailanthus* survives. There will always be more.

And this is something Kuroda knows. When he stares out at the country, when he stands with his binoculars for minutes at a time, I think this is what he sees.

In the night I look up at him. His eyes shine back at me. I

wonder what they're seeing when they gaze into the future. That is what concerns me most. I wonder if they see me; I wonder if they see his wife. I wonder if they see a great distance, if they see the cherry trees instead of millet and bamboo.

But we never discuss it, never; we pretend it doesn't matter. If you were there, under the bed, you wouldn't know we even cared. In a way this pact of silence is the oddest thing of all but it is also very natural. I feel both ways; sometimes I badly want to make him listen while I say it but then again I want to seal my own mouth shut, to forget my Japanese, to cut out my tongue so that I can never, ever, ever utter a word.

The night before last, as we lay there, still breathing quickly, I almost spoke to him. There was something about the way he had taken me that evening, something so devoted and gentle and reserved about the way he had come into me that I was filled when we were done with a sense of regard, overwhelmed by the recognition that I understood and appreciated him, that I admired him so much. That his attention—his affection—meant more to me than I had allowed myself to know. For the first time I wanted him to look after me, to take care of me. I wanted him to shape my life. These thoughts led directly to panic at the idea of losing him, to crazy longing for a promise that we would never be apart, never again for a moment, and I reached out and took him in my hand and caressed him, wanting only to be joined to him again. I saw him start in surprise and I knew he might not like it but I also felt his rhythm in my palm, the steady flow of blood, and I did what I had never done before. I was wild, like an animal; I held nothing in reserve. When he was ready I climbed onto him and I knew he would be lost in me,

I could tell by his movements and his small sounds and the tension in his flesh that I was taking him somewhere entirely new, transforming him, and I clung to his body and concentrated on the doing of this for him, the mission I'd set out on, the precious gift he waited to receive. I tried desperately to pursue him, to encircle him; I wanted to satisfy every longing, every hope he'd ever had. I seemed to know what was required. My own eyes opened in amazement, my body shivered in delight, and in the end he groaned and spent himself and I was pitifully happy, washed with joy and gratitude for what I had accomplished. It was almost a condition of new innocence, or grace. I was so thoroughly content that it took me several seconds to begin to marvel at myself, to be astonished by what had happened, what I'd felt, what I'd done. I was so weary I thought I might die.

I almost spoke to him then. I didn't know what I would say but my mouth was partly open when the gunfire began. At the very first shot he pushed me off and rolled to the floor, pulling me down with him, but when he realized it was coming from some distance away he got up and put on his pants and boots and took his gun and went outside. The shooting continued in fits and starts and I lay unmoving on the floor, cold and uncomfortable on the hard surface, incapable of using a single muscle. I could barely believe he had rushed out like that but I knew he'd had no choice. To worry that they would kill him was beyond me, to fear for my own safety was totally impossible. My contribution was to lie there. I almost lost consciousness; I was dreamy and wandering, only partly aware of the sounds from outside. I tried within it all to retrieve what had just happened and was rushing away from me, to bring back and preserve its every aspect, but the harder I tried, the more I found that there were only two things: the shock of the pleasure that my body had achieved and the surprising depth and vigor of my feelings for him. That was all. Those two things. I knew I did not love him, not the way he loved me, but I could see I'd gotten closer. And I knew without doubt that I was truly a woman, and that I'd made him my man.

In a minute or two the firing tapered off, and then it stopped altogether. I heard his voice in the yard, giving orders, and I heard the lieutenant and several others as well. They walked together in a group; I was afraid he would bring them into the building but they moved past. Though still barely awake I wanted to wait for him—I was getting worried, although I'd heard him speak, worried that he was wounded, that something drastic had happened—and I determined to stand up. Very slowly and unsteadily I managed this, and then sat cross-legged on the bed. As I waited my happiness began to drain away, and with a silent cry I let it go. I ached for it but knew I couldn't keep it with me. I was sitting that way without once having moved when he finally arrived: my old self again, almost but not quite, a little distant, a little angry, but with a new piece added to me. I think when he looked at me he knew.

"What was it?" I asked.

He sat down on the bed. I wanted him to hold me and I wanted him to go. He was a stranger and someone I had known all my life; he was a flower and a devil. He was a dwarf, a beast soldier, he was my ancestor, my child.

"Nothing," he told me. "It was nothing." He drew a breath. "One of the sentries imagined voices and started firing. And then the others joined in. It was stupid of them to keep it up for so long, a foolish waste of ammunition, but I can't really blame them. They're so bored and so tense from waiting endlessly here that no one could have stopped them from making a commotion." He looked somberly at me. "I suppose they were having fun."

"I am glad," I said to him, in a weakened voice I hardly recognized, "that there was no danger. I am glad you are unhurt." I felt my fingers on my knees. "I am glad you have come back to me."

He sat silently on the edge of the bed, his feet on the floor, his hands resting on either side of him, looking down. "You really should not have that worry," he said, almost casually, almost teasing. "I will always do that."

We waited together. It was seconds, I know, just a few seconds, but it might have been hours. Finally—when I'd despaired of it—he took me in his arms. My tears and moans began then and I hid my face in his neck and shoulder, ashamed, trying to keep quiet, stifling the sobs and whispers and whimpers that came and came and came.

"I want you to sleep in here with me from now on," he said at last. "I don't want you out there by yourself, on the floor."

Damn him. Damn him. I can't stand this. It has to finish soon. Why won't he leave me and have done with it? Why won't he cut me loose? I am very frightened, very, more frightened than I've ever been, and I'm sure he's frightened too. He is a realistic man. He knows as well as I do that nothing good can come of this, nothing, that with every day together we go another step further from hope, another step toward doom, another step into the crater of the volcano. He knows as well as I that he can't have me. Not for long.

TWENTY ONE

I knew she would not like it. I half expected her to laugh at me. There was no laughter—I was grateful—but she could hardly believe what she was hearing. Granted it was startling, even bizarre, but I had thought it through to the end. I had thought it through and thought it through until I could not think any more. One thing my father taught me, one good thing, was to consider every possibility, to look at every way out. To examine each option in turn so that you arrive, sooner or later, at your answer. You have three good choices left, you find, or two or one, or none. And then you can decide.

She was eating, in that huddled way she has, while I sat without moving behind my bowl of eggs and rice. To my surprise I was quite nervous about telling her; my hands were trembling slightly. As much as she means to me she had never made me tremble before, not that way, but my anxiety was such that I was actually nauseated, and could not think of eating my dinner. I had no choice but to begin.

"I want to send you to Japan," I said.

She looked up from her bowl and stared at me. Her eyes were very dark. The sticks were halfway to her mouth, her torso bent, her head tilted back so she could see.

"It's not as silly as it sounds," I said. "I'm an officer, don't forget, a captain. And I have many friends at home. There are things I can arrange."

She looked down and began to eat again, the long sticks moving metrically from bowl to mouth and back. She never gobbles her food but she always eats steadily and doesn't stop until she is finished. It could be a recent habit—it could have something to do with all the time she spent hungry, before she came here—but I would guess if I had to that she always ate like that. It seems so practiced. She eats a lot at every meal, at least with me, and if she is still thin it is a healthy thinness, maybe thinner than she once was but without the look of a victim. She doesn't eat that way from hunger; she does it because it suits her.

"I can't imagine how that would work," she said, after taking several mouthfuls.

"Getting you out of here is the hardest," I told her. "I'm still thinking about that." I wished she would stop eating and let me see her face. "Your passage from Shanghai I believe I can manage, and taking care of you when you get there is the easiest of all. Once you step onto the dock you will be safe."

She paused and looked at me again, the sticks this time at

rest in the bowl, though she still held them. The sleeve of her other arm she raised to her lips.

"Something tells me your wife and colleagues will not be happy to do you this favor," she said.

"No," I said. "They won't." I forced myself to pick up my own utensils and shifted the eggs around on my rice. "But there are others who can help. I have friends in Nagasaki who are loyal only to me, who don't even know my family. They will look after you."

"Because you tell them to?" she asked.

"Just because."

"Without any questions?"

"Without any questions."

She shook her head briefly and started eating again. I watched the lamp's light glowing on her face, on her smooth skin, and also in her hair. I tried to guess at her feelings. Several gaijin have confessed to me that they cannot read our faces but compared to the Chinese we are transparent as the day. When they decide you should not know something you do not know it. They keep it from you with shuttered windows, with a locked and bolted door.

I sought patience; I thought she needed time to get used to it. There was nothing to do but have a mouthful of my dinner. It was very good, as is most of what she makes, and it was still very warm. As I chewed I had a sudden wish for coffee, real coffee, like what I used to drink at the university, a keener longing than I've had for anything since I came here. There was a young man in my dormitory who was devoted to good coffee and always knew where to get it—to get a really good cup—and he would often take me with him. Though I was never as enthusiastic as he I did learn to enjoy it, enough so that even after he was gone I occasionally went out for a cup on my own. It was a very expensive habit and once I left there it faded. But sometimes when I drink our barley tea I imagine it is coffee in my hand; I listen for his high-pitched voice. In an odd way it brings back my youth.

"Will I see you," she asked, "when you come back from the war?"

I watched her face. "That is a long way off," I said. "Who knows if I'll come back at all? Who knows where you will be? I can't even guess how long they'll keep me here."

"Will I see you?" she asked.

I closed my eyes then and held my hands tightly over them. "Yes," I said from behind my palms. "Yes, if there is any way for me to do it. If I am alive I will come to you."

When I looked at her again she was finishing her food. With skillful motions she lifted the last grains of rice out of the bottom of the bowl.

"What about the people there?" she asked. "Will they hate me because I'm Chinese?"

"Some will hate you. Many will look down on you. No one will harm you if you're careful. It will help that you're a woman and that you speak Japanese." I hesitated. "You might even get some assistance from the government," I said, "on account of your grandmother. Do you remember her full name?"

She stared at me.

"If you are careful in what you do and say," I said, "and you follow my friends' instructions, no one will harm you."

Her bowl was empty; she laid her sticks down beside it and wiped her mouth again, put her elbows on the table and her chin on her hands. She looked so beautiful to me then that I wanted to die. I truly wanted to die, then and there, so I would never have to look at another sight again. She was lovely. She was everything I desired.

"Why must this happen?"

"It is the only way to save you."

"And why would you want to?"

"If I cannot save myself—"

She stood and took her bowl to the basin. "Oh, Kuroda," she said, sighing and actually smiling at me before turning away, just for an instant but with a measured affection that caused me searing pain, "I wish I could believe you. I wish I could believe that it was possible or even desirable but I can't. I can't. I know you understand why."

"Please think it over," I said.

"I will but it won't change my mind."

"You are all I care about."

She turned and stood with her back to the basin, her hands behind her, her eyes on my face. "I am sorry," she said.

I threw my bowl to the floor.

"I meant," she said a moment later, as she was cleaning up the mess, "not why would you want to, but to what end?" She paused and looked up at me. "What would be the purpose of it?"

It was the raid the other night that made me ask her. That's what has me grasping at straws. Else I might have been more clever, less obvious, might have tried a different approach. Before then I had all sorts of fantasies about Li's future and mine but now, for the first time, I fully realize the danger. Now the danger makes me urgent and the fantasies are real. I must do something. If she won't agree to one plan

I will convince her of another, whether she likes it or not, and if I have to I will force her. But my time is running short. I've got to get her out of here.

I wish I knew why they let us drive them off so easily; they could have made for bad trouble. I can't imagine why they went. From what Ashizawa said there were a lot of them, possibly enough to overrun us. (All on foot, he claims, though I have pictured them on horseback.) Thank god for Nagai's thought about the flares; if Ashizawa hadn't had one they might never have stopped. In its light he saw them coming by the dozens, he said, by the hundreds, and though I know he was exaggerating Sakoda backed him up. I do not think that there were hundreds of them but dozens is quite possible, yes. They could have hurt us very badly. They were naked in the light—there was nowhere for them to hide—but when it died they could have kept coming. They could have sprinted up the hill. There was no second flare but even if there had been they could have reached our perimeter before we were organized. Some of them would surely have been killed but they might have done away with us. I can't understand why they didn't try.

Sakoda says he saw machine guns. But Ashizawa talks of pikes.

I should have expected this. I am a buffoon, I admit it, a blind man. I am comic. If I were not so afraid it would amuse me to think of how I cursed them for leaving me here, as if the point were to humiliate me. As if it were my punishment. All that time I was crying to myself when I should have been angry, I should have hated them for exposing me like this to so little benefit, for risking my life. *For experimenting on me*. The faithless dogs. I can hear them if I listen:

"Let us see how long they can hold on out there; it will be useful information. Care to have a wager on it?"

I am a proud man, yes. I am as brave as I should be and my men are braver still. But we have done nothing. Nothing! No wonder they despise me. They blame me for their presence here and also for not protecting them. I won't let them search the countryside, I won't let them drink and whore, I won't let them hurt the locals. All I will allow them is to eat and sleep and drill and stand guard and wait for the Chinese to come for them, and now the Chinese have come and nothing has changed; they have nothing even to hope for. It is no way for a Japanese man to live. I marvel that they have not mutinied, or run away. I probably would if it were me.

I'm at the center of a storm; this has become very serious. To lose the bridge was bad enough but we must defend the garrison. I must determine how to do it. If we fight poorly they will kill us all, and if we fight well but not well enough—if we are left at half our strength and the colonel will not rescue us, if our distress calls to go unanswered—the troops will become so disloyal to me that I won't be safe. Li won't be safe. I have done more to them than they can forgive me for, I think, and dare not add another failure.

I must be smart now, it is clear. I must be hard. I must employ Nagai's advice. I must gather everything I learned from my father, from my training, from all my war experience to get us through this situation. We are caught, *I* am caught between two enemies—the guerrillas and my men, the Chinese and the Imperial Army—and far from saving Li I have no plan for my own survival, not even for another day, another week. One side or the other will find a way to do me in. One or the other will condemn me.

This could be panic, I suppose. These could be meaningless forebodings. Certainly I am narcissistic; they risked my life by placing me here but it could not have been personal, they don't know me from a gingko tree. Perhaps I have less to fear than I suspect, from both the Chinese and my men. Perhaps I'm weaker than I know.

In another month they might relieve us. They might send us to Peking or Hangchow. In a month or two there could be a truce—even the communists might lay down their arms. Anything is possible. But my intuition tells me that the danger is very grave. I have a native sort of wisdom that aids me more than all my training, all my books; my ancestors are with me now, I think, and my ancestors know. They have fought in many wars, many battles. And they don't like what they see.

She doesn't know we were attacked. I hid the truth, deliberately. I didn't want to scare her. When I heard that first shot I welcomed it; lying there with her was almost more than I could bear. I was beside myself with feeling and if the intruders hadn't come I probably would have risen in a minute or two and gone to sit in the other room, or to stand out in the yard. My bliss, my desperation, my confusion and my grief were such at just that moment that I valued nothing more than the battle and my enemy. I honored conflict. I wanted to be with my men, my countrymen, I wanted to be my Emperor's subject. So I flew quickly out the door.

But I couldn't escape, not that way. As time went by and the crisis faded one thought was in my mind, one thought only: Li, Li, Li. *Protect Li, defend Li*. Giving orders I struggled not to say her name; as I went through the camp with Nagai and the others it is was all I could do to keep from rushing back to her. *You must be strong*, my soul commanded, *you must endure to shelter Li*. I knew she was sitting there frightened and silent, waiting to hear, and all I wanted was to tell her. I wanted to share every detail. But I could not show this to the men; I had to make the right impression. So I worked very hard until I thought I had convinced them, and then at last I could return.

She would not ask me when I got there. She sat on the bed and looked at me, like a well-behaved child, and refused. I wanted her to but she would not. When I told her it was nothing it didn't ease her as I'd hoped, didn't change her; she was as she'd been before. Very solemn and most still. I felt terrible for lying but it was what I had decided.

"I am happy," she said when I was done, "that you are safe. I am happy to see you again." And then I knew I had not dreamt it.

TWENTY TWO

I wonder if he has lost his mind. It seems possible, even likely; the conditions in which he lives are not particularly sane. His load is heavy, he faces hardship in every hour of every day, and he has no one to share his troubles with. He is almost entirely alone. The truth is that he is more alone than I am, strange as that may be, for while I have him he does not, in the same sense, have me.

I don't know what it would be like under different circumstances, if we had come together in Tokyo or Shanghai. Maybe I'd be warmer and give more to him then. But its as likely that he wouldn't care at all about me. We are creatures of just one habit, he and I, an event with just one place, and the image of us entwined in any room other than this room, on any bed other than this bed, is ever dimmer and more distant as the days and nights go by.

I would like to do well by him—I would like to give freely—but I have no resources. I have no influence. I can't protect him from danger; I can't provide for him; I can't lift him and carry him when he's afraid. I know my presence, my affection, my body mean the world to him but I feel like a bystander, almost, I feel incidental, like a courier who brings something long awaited and then stands silently aside.

All of this makes me sad, I admit. It makes me yearn for once to be powerful and brave, to have been born of different fortune. But even more I rue the limits of the woman that I am. I regret my incapacities. I am not a good choice; it was his bad luck to fall in with me, bad luck and bad sense, for which I'm sorry. I feel for him, yes, but what I feel is not enough, not in proportion, and I would like to do better. I would like to truly love him.

So I must blame myself as well when I worry about his sanity. And worry is what I do, worry and fret; I feel guilt but no assurance. I wonder about his intentions; I speculate; I ask if I could ever really know a Japanese. I wonder if he is weakening, I wonder if he has lost his mind and I wonder—I don't want to but I do—if he is embracing despair. If he will give up trying soon. The Li who lives inside me and wants badly to survive is horrified by that, and indignant, but the rest of me doesn't mind. Giving up and waiting for the worst—maybe that would bring me freedom. Maybe I could be generous then. The odds are rotten anyway, we're as good as dead, so maybe it would be best to stop my struggling and let go, to accept the certain end that some high heaven has decreed and try to discover in it something valuable, a blessing, something noble and new.

Fine words, those. Fine sentiments for Li. But it really does scare me, the thought that he'll give up; I can't pretend it doesn't. It makes me ever more desperate to somehow force myself to act, to leave this place, and at the same time more determined to stay with him always. I've found at this late date a fresh and growing fear of pain, or an ancient one I can no longer ignore; the idea of violation and bodily harm now fills me with terror. But so does the prospect of losing him. If I go or if I stay I face both of these futures, they are bound together, therefore I have reason to do neither. My being rests in perfect balance and what tips it just enough, what keeps me here and not in Hupeh is the fact that he needs me, he relies on me; without me he'd surely fall. I may not be capable of loving a person but at least I have my honor and I repay all my debts. I do my duty very well.

"I can't imagine why you haven't left me," he said one afternoon, as I was hanging up his laundry.

"It is not necessary to imagine it," I told him. " You see me right before your eyes."

I'm not the only one who holds back, I'm very certain; there are things he keeps from me. Words he will not say. I know, for example, that he lied about the raid. I know I heard two sets of guns. That is one of the things that is dragging him under, both the raid itself and the lie. There is surely someone out there and he knows he can't get rid of them. They'll be back. It seems he is finally accepting this—acknowledging that he is a foreign soldier in extremely hostile country, country over which he has almost no control—but he still can't say so to me. He'll reach that point eventually, I hope, if we last long enough, but I don't know that we will. I believe it's a matter of weeks now, or even days. I don't think we have much time.

I would hurry him along if I could but it's not possible. I have done what I can do to draw him out and now must wait. I must wait for him to trust me. I want to force him, I want to say Kuroda, Kuroda, I'm your one and only friend, but I have done all that I can. I'm at my limit of my tolerance, I've discovered—for obligation, for engagement, for stiff and awkward give-and-take—and I'm just barely holding on. If we are truly to be comrades it will have to start with him; he must leave them at last, of his own free will, and come over to my side.

I know we don't have much time. No real reason to believe that but it's a hunch I can't deny. I have the sense that there are changes pursuing us, overtaking us, that we are at the center of a swiftly closing net. It isn't just the guerrillas; there are other signs and omens that speak of everything we're prey to. I would have hoped I'd be insensible to shock by now—I would have assumed it—but it turns out that I'm not and there are shocks at every turn. I'm as jumpy as I always was at New Year, as a child, spooked by noise and candle flames and dragons in the night.

The lieutenant speaks Chinese. He always has. That is one cold harsh reality; it makes me terribly upset. When I told it to Kuroda it didn't come as a surprise. I don't know why it bothers me so much but it does; I find it sinister, both the fact and Kuroda's silent knowledge of it. There is nothing so remarkable about his knowing Chinese—I'm sure that many of them do—and it doesn't make it easier for him to harm me, I don't think, but it drops the bottom out somehow and forces me to look on any notion of security, even that which I feel when I stand by the stove or hold tight to Kuroda's back in the darkness, as an empty silly farce.

I was walking from the well to the schoolhouse when he stopped me. I was carrying a bucket of water. He stood right in my path to block my progress and at first I refused to put my burden down, I even tried to step by him, but I couldn't and the bucket was very heavy. Soon I had to drop it. I let it fall an inch or two to the grass between my toes and then stared down into the water, waiting for him, trying to conjure goldfish from the faint gleams of sunlight that were swimming below the surface.

"Perhaps you'd like someone to help you with that," he said. His tone was respectful and polite. I was so very surprised by this and by his saying it in Chinese—he even spoke in a Kiangsu dialect and he spoke it easily, flawlessly, I think to show me what he knew and what he was capable of—that I started and almost looked up. But my distaste for and a horror of his ugly, hateful face kept my eyes on the bucket. I felt my back and shoulders twitch and I knew I would start trembling. Of all of them he turns my heart the coldest.

"No, thank you," I said. "I do it daily and it isn't very far."

"No, thank you, *sir*," he told me, still mild. Then I did look up, and found him smiling at me in a peculiar way. I wasn't actually sure it was a smile, though it resembled one; I didn't even know if I was seeing his features as they really were. His face is so dark, so scarred, and his glasses hide his eyes. But it seemed to be a grin, though there was little pleasure in it, and it persisted as he watched me, as we stood confronting each other.

"No, thank you, Lieutenant," I said in Japanese. I thought

it would be best to simply wait for his dismissal; with an expression like that he was liable to do anything. So I stood there with my head down, motionless in the sunshine, my hands folded together so he wouldn't see them shake.

"I want to show you something," he said. I looked up as he reached into his pocket. When he brought out a photograph I was astonished—would he really show his loved ones to a filthy Chinese prostitute?—but I could have saved my disbelief. It wasn't a picture of his wife or his children, or of his parents or his sweetheart or his hometown in Japan. It was a picture of him raping a woman. An older Chinese woman, dirty and naked on the ground. Her eyes spoke of the pain. Some other man's hand was thrust into her mouth and Nagai's were on her biceps, pinning her to the earth, though it was clear that she'd stopped struggling long before.

He pushed it closer to my face. I smelled a strong smell of oil, of soap and tobacco. "I have a long list in my tent," he said, his voice still tranquil. "With dates and places and even some names. Do you want to see that too?"

As I related this to Kuroda he hardly stirred. I thought he would be angered but he wasn't. Beyond my outrage I had questions—who is this man, what is he doing here?—but I didn't dare to ask them, so I just repeated the conversation. When I finished he sighed and looked put out, not ashamed or embarrassed, exactly, but like a man who is forced to masquerade as something he can't be. "Believe me," he said, speaking quietly and evenly, "when I tell you that I would like to send him away. I would like to see him gone." He closed his eyes. "But I need him," he said. "I must have him. It's men like him who win the wars."

I agree that this is true, perhaps much truer than he realizes.

Another matter that concerns me—I have not shared it with Kuroda—is the state of my health. I think I may be ill. I'm not sure what it is; I don't believe I have a fever but my head aches. My chest is sore. My stomach's painful or unsettled and at times I lose my balance. I have always been healthy since my first day on earth, I made it through those weeks of hunger without ever getting sick, but I can't keep on ignoring this; it nags at me each hour like something started but undone. I'm unaccustomed to infirmity. I may be perfectly well, this may be just a figment, a made-up solution to my problems, but something is different. My body feels different. It is a change I can't ignore.

And in the world, out in the world, beyond this hilltop. Beyond these walls. There is wild news in the village, so wild they even told the traitor. So wild they spoke aloud instead of whispering. It is such huge and timeless news that it draws us together, makes us Chinese and no more, leads us to crouch in the dirt and mutter, and shiver, and be thankful for the accidents of our births.

The Huang Ho has burst its dikes, they say. No one can remember a bigger flood. Huaipei is now a lake and most of northern Honan too, and all that water and debris is washing into the Huai Ho, overflowing it in turn and moving south towards us. They say a Japanese army was drowned in it. They say the Huai will never be the same. And we are next, they are certain—the waters will be here in a day or two. They'll sweep over us. Those in the valleys will never survive.

I asked one woman why she did not flee. She looked at me with pity and said, "Goodness, girl, where to?"

It is so threatening, this disaster, so unexpectedly large. Even at a distance. Even in the face of more immediate concerns. Not that big floods are anything new, not that I believe the crazy tales—I believe there is a flood, a bad flood, but not that all China south of the Huang is going under water—but it adds a level to my fear, a sharper quality. It reaches a haunted place deep in my being.

I have no feeling for the victims, or their ghosts; I don't know them and it's hard for me to imagine their suffering. In fact it seems so peaceful when I think of it, all that water spreading slowly across the vast and silent land. So very calm. But ghosts are ghosts and a flood is a flood; this is tradition, almost culture, a time of mourning for us all.

And I am not above it, not in the slightest. I can't help the way it makes me feel and I wouldn't want to try. I was born here, after all, the Chinese child of Chinese parents and of all those before them and as such I believe, I know, I am convinced of two things: that our affairs are less than nothing as compared to those of heaven and that when we forget this—when we begin to think the world was made by men—heaven hastens to put us right. To humble us. Whatever answers the books provide, whatever science we learn, these things remain essentially true. I can't forget them. For all my years of education I am a peasant at the bottom, a frightened peasant just the same as the villagers, and I can see what they see now: that we have surely been warned.

TWENTY THREE

The knife blade entered like a ghost. I hardly knew it was in me. It came to me like sunlight, like bird calls, like the faint smell of sesame, and it left the same way.

We were alone; he caught me walking in the very early morning. Somehow the sentries missed him. His feet were bare and made no sound and he was wearing a Japanese corporal's tunic, which may also have helped. I do not think he was Han Chinese; maybe Manchurian, maybe Korean. I never got a good look at him, and disease and poverty make peasant faces nondescript. His was rugged and impassive, even as he stabbed me, with not a sign of human feeling. He might have been felling a tree.

In any case he is dead now. They heard my cry and shot him four times, almost before he was through with me. He died instantly; it meant that Nagai could not question him but I suppose if they had held their fire he would have stabbed me again.

I have been here before. It is familiar, though also new. Penetrated by a stranger—perhaps now I understand. That is what has happened to me, isn't it? The same as what happened to all of them, those long months ago, what almost happened to Li. Perhaps this is the price I pay for all my anguished inaction, my pointless sympathy. I am condemned to join those women, to be a victim just like them because I would not try to help.

We have no doctor with us. There is only a young medic, barely skilled, and it never occurred to me to wonder why. They brought me to my bed and laid me on it—I saw Li standing in the doorway with a horrified look, she was asleep when I got up but the shots must have awakened her—and Amano examined the wound. It wasn't very bloody and he told me it looked clean. I was faint but alert, and I noticed when he touched it that there was very little pain. There was more sensation at the limit of the wound, at the deepest point the knife had reached, than there was at the surface. Or at least it seemed that way; perhaps I just imagined it.

"Can you tell which organs might be damaged?" I asked. "From the location of the cut?"

"I don't think so, Captain," he said. I was surprised by his calm tone. "We're going to have to wait and see." I felt a tugging at my skin as he cleaned me. "But I think you'll be OK, sir, I don't believe you need to worry. You're lucky that he didn't get your lungs or your heart."

Li stood against one wall as Amano took my pulse again,

and Nagai against another. She kept her eyes on me; his were fixed on her. Outside I heard a sergeant, shouting hoarsely at the men.

"I gather," I said to Amano, before he put the bandage on, "that the blade was very sharp."

"Oh yes sir," he said. "It's quite a neat cut. Do you want to raise your head and look?"

"No, thank you," I said. "Go ahead and cover it." As he worked I turned to Nagai. "Lieutenant," I told him, "my servant is to stay here with me at all times. Under no circumstances is she to be removed from this room." His face was blank, but I thought I saw him stand a little straighter. "She will be nursing me. And you will give her what she asks for. When I wake I expect to find her here." Suddenly I had to cough and then the wound did hurt, it hurt very much. I held myself still and in a moment it subsided. "Do you understand?"

"What about Amano?" he asked.

"He will tend to me as he sees fit. She will help him."

"Yes, sir," said the lieutenant.

"You understand?"

"Kuroda-dono, I do."

I thought of the assassin as I lay there. I wondered about him. Was he a partisan? A lunatic? Did he attack me out of politics or was it simple revenge? No way of telling now but whatever his reasons he can't have hoped to get away. He knew he would be killed, probably before he could do harm. He didn't even have a gun; it was luck, pure blind luck that led his knife to such a target. When he saw me he must have been elated. Because he would therefore be dying a hero, a martyr. Or perhaps it didn't matter to him, perhaps he didn't know me or was incapable of caring. It could be he just stabbed the first beast soldier he could get to.

I remember now that he spoke to me. I believe he whispered "monster" as he pushed the long blade forward. How peculiar—another who knew Japanese. You'd think the odds would be against it. The country must be full of them, or they in some way come to me.

"Do you want the morphine, Captain?"

"Not yet, but get it ready. If I need it I will tell you."

When Nagai left the room, Li moved to the head of my bed and sat there in a chair, watching me, giving me sips of water, wiping my forehead when I asked her to. I drifted in and out of sleep, or something like sleep; I was tired, very tired, but not in pain for the most part. As long as I did not move. She sat over me and answered when I spoke, although she tried to discourage me, and the corporal rested in a chair in the corner—humbled, I think, by his sense of duty, and the knowledge that there was no further aid he could give.

I like Amano. He is good to me. The other soldiers are glad, I would guess, even Nagai, probably even Yawata. They all want me to die but he wants me to live. He respects me. He is curious and hopeful about the progress of my wound but is content to wait for results. He is a good soldier. I wish I could reward him. I might make him a sergeant if I get the chance.

But I won't, unfortunately; he is wrong, I am dying. I am quite certain. I knew it from the beginning. He doesn't know it but how could he? Li doesn't know, or if she knows she won't face it. I cannot blame her; it must not be very pleasant for her to think along those lines. But she really has no reason to be worried. Later, when Nagai comes back—if

I feel myself going I will make them call him for me—I will force him to pledge on his honor to protect her. As a man I don't trust him but I think he is a decent Japanese in this sense, a decent officer. If he makes me a promise he will keep it, and I think I can persuade him to promise. He will see that she is not harmed.

At one point I opened my eyes to find her gazing at me, enormously sad, thinking not of herself but entirely—I am sure of this, I am very sure—of me. I could see grief growing in her, growing and blossoming like a flower. I wanted to give comfort but I knew that wasn't possible; there were no such words available. I tried to find them all the same.

"I wish for your father," I said. I think I meant it as a joke. Her face became even sadder, of course, sadder than I would have believed, and she started to cry. The gentle tears ran down her cheeks. Amano sat quietly in his corner.

"Don't cry," I told her. "I'm sorry. Don't cry." It shamed me to have said that; it pained me that I hadn't the strength to wipe her tears. I wanted to embrace her but she would not even touch me.

"And I," she answered softly, "I wish for yours."

It was peaceful through the day. There were a few shouts and thuds and other noises from the yard, but it seemed that Nagai was mostly keeping the men quiet. My condition became neither better nor worse. The medic took my pulse occasionally, he felt my side and took my temperature, and after some time—I don't know how long because I kept coming and going—he told Li to boil more water and then gave me a new dressing. He said the wound still looked very good but it was too early to tell; I wondered if this was the truth but I knew he was all I had. It began to seem very odd that there was so little pain, I almost wanted to pretend there was more, but when he offered me the drug I told him no.

Through all of this she stayed; she never even left her chair. I felt her presence and was comforted.

Late in the afternoon, when the light began to change, Major Suzuki came to visit. At first it surprised me but then I asked why it had taken him so long, until the ending of the day. He is dead, poor Suzuki, and now so am I; soon I will be with him. If not in some afterlife, some incorporeal realm, then at least in his journey home from China to Japan. My ashes will follow his, perhaps go on the same ship if they save them up in batches. I hope he is still waiting in Shanghai, on the docks; it hasn't been so long since he was killed and he might be. I would be honored to be with him on the trip across the sea.

A few days after he died, after the messenger came, we got a report that Hsuchow had fallen. I remembered his prediction and I tried to fix the dates, but it was hard to do precisely and I had no way of knowing whether or not he'd heard the news. I never found out where he was at the time—it might have been some outpost even more remote than here—so I couldn't be sure.

Did he know about Hsuchow before they killed him? And if he did, did it please him? Did it soothe him at the end?

They should not have given up, those Chinese soldiers at Nanking. They should not have kept retreating the way they did; they should never have surrendered. At Shanghai at least they fought us, and at Hsuchow too, at Taierchuang. But not at Nanking. It was they who condemned the women of the city, not me, not Japan, condemned the women and themselves; if they had fought on to the end our own men would have found restraint. We would not have been so eager to punish, to degrade. I know we were encouraged by the high command, I am not stupid or naive, but still it would have meant something. To all the men. If they had fought us for their honor it might not have ended that way.

Because surrender is weakness. And weakness is death.

I wanted to explain to Li about my ashes, about going home. I tried to but she didn't want to hear it. I phrased it incidentally, as an interesting thought; I told her, "Oh, by the way, here is something you should know," but she simply would not listen.

"Hush," she said. "Please try to sleep."

So I gave up rather easily. What earthly difference did it make?

All those thoughts about Suzuki, about our journey to the homeland, brought me gradually to my family. In the twilight I remembered them. I was astonished to consider how long it had been, not only since I'd seen them but since I'd even thought of them, or wondered how they were. My daughter is very much older now, of course; I might not know her if I saw her. Girls change a lot at certain ages. My wife probably looks a good deal worse, she never stood worry well and I would think that my absence has aged her. I haven't heard from her in a very long time but I'm certain she has written, and my uncle and mother too; the army is keeping their letters from me. They must be asking what has happened. They must be thinking I am dead.

Well, by now they're right or nearly so. It's too bad I can't send them all one final message.

I had an insight then about the ones at home, a thought I

could never have had when I was whole. As I lay there half-awake, listening to Li cooking supper for Amano and herself, watching the shadows, I was hit by a startling idea. Suddenly I realized: *They don't know what is happening here.* Of course the papers don't report it. They probably think I'm doing good. If my father lives on he is proud of me, proud, and my mother and wife and daughter accept their deprivation for the good of the country, for the good of the Chinese, for history. They may even boast about me. My god. What a horror, that they don't know what we've done here. What an absolute horror. What a monument of shame.

I was surprised when the supper smell came to my nostrils—I had forgotten about everything but myself—and as it did it made me hungry. And being hungry made me hurt. I looked into the glowing lamp and tried to will the pain away but I couldn't; it was rapidly much worse. It was as if I had been able to lock up my insides, to keep them rigid, but then could not fend off the smell of the food that called to them of what they really were, of their fundamental nature. At that moment they all started working again and I couldn't prevent them. My resolution came to naught.

And then they hurt me. They hurt me. They burned me like fire.

Li and Amano were eating by the stove. I said, "I need some morphine now, Corporal," and both rushed to my side. I was impressed by the speed with which they approached me; it seemed they were there in a particle of an instant.

"I'm sorry, sir," said Amano, wiping my arm. "I hope I didn't wait too long." He had the hypodermic ready, but as he lifted it I found the strength to raise my hand and hold him.

"Just a little," I said. "Just a very little. As little as you think will give me some relief."

It surely seemed like very little (I watched the plunger as he pushed it) but it changed me. It clouded me. For a time I was not with them; I was in another room, another country, in some other foreign war. It was familiar there, almost, not the strange taste in my mouth and the ringing in my ears but the absence of direction and of gravity, the redefinition of space. Although I have seldom been delirious and have never been drugged it was familiar. I was not afraid. But while it was curious, enjoyable—it eased my distress—I wanted to be rid of it. I didn't want to give my last few hours to morphine, I realized; I wanted to be with Li.

I had almost let go to sink down into the stupor but her image pulled me back. It filled me with such sharp and painful heartache, painful even through my fog, that I was ashamed of myself—for cowardice, for denying that I loved her, for trying to lock up those other insides too—and I wanted to weep. I struggled back to the world, thinking of her, cursing the bitter cruelty of having stumbled on this woman in the bottom of a pit, in a trap with no way out, and of the fact that I would lose her. Having found her in a barnyard I was losing her forever, in a schoolhouse on a hill. I wanted badly not to go. I felt for my feet, to plant them firmly on whatever was beneath them. I wanted to see her again.

When I came to myself the room was dark and very quiet. The lamp had been turned to its lowest setting and I noticed the red glow of the stove. Li and Amano were asleep. My side hurt, but it was a different kind of pain from before, the kind unaffected by breathing and swallowing and other small movements. It was only an incision in my abdomen now, only a mortal wound; I could lie there and endure it without trying to hold it back. It wasn't something that could rule me.

I stared up at the ceiling. Why does Nagai not return to me? I asked it. What keeps him away for so long? It chills me to believe that he doesn't even care. Is he never going to come? Is he really going to leave and let me die here in this bed, without showing his respect? I would not treat him that way.

Then I saw Li. She wasn't asleep; she was sitting to my right. She had been there all along. Her eyes were open and she was watching me. I knew she would not sleep until I died. Slowly and carefully I pulled my arm out from under the blanket and put my hand in her lap, where hers already rested, and she held it for me. Her soft warm skin was on mine. I was so grateful, so grateful to her. I adored her. I closed my eyes and trembled. I knew then that I was happy, that I had become as happy as I might ever have hoped to become, that nothing mattered anymore. It was an easy end for me. The only sadness was for her, that I could no longer protect her or provide for her. For myself I wanted nothing. All that mattered was her future.

"In the morning I'll tell Amano to bring the lieutenant here," I whispered. "I will make sure they do not hurt you."

"Thank you," she replied.

"There's no way to be certain but if you choose your moment carefully I'm sure you can get away, get away entirely. There aren't enough of us out here to cause you problems. If you can find the guerrillas they'll look after you."

"I know," she whispered. "I think that's what I'll do."

I heard the medic's steady breathing from the corner. He hadn't stirred. "I cherish you," I said, not really whispering anymore but still speaking very softly. "I wish I didn't have to go."

"Kuroda," she said, "you are an agent of heaven. That is what I believe." She squeezed my hand. "But I never deserved you."

Then she sat and watched me weep.

I must tell her, I know that. I am steadied and determined. It is the one thing left to do. I have decided that she should hear the truth; she had better know, before I die. If she survives she'll find out sooner or later, from someone or someone else, and she'll wonder if I was there. She'll wonder what I did, what part I had. It is important to be honest with her; when she remembers this valley, when she looks back on our days here, I don't want her doubting me. I want her to know that I gave her everything.

So I will tell her now. Not the details, she doesn't need them, but I will draw the broadest outlines. I think I have enough control. I will tell her and it will hurt and she will hate me, even if she loves me she will hate me, but then I will be satisfied. And then I can rest.

TWENTY FOUR

He is dead. How did this happen?

How did I come to this place, with all these burdens? It seems so simple, so impossible. Like a folktale or a dream.

I am weeping as I walk. I am unused to it. I can see just well enough to go on. My face and the shirt I stole are wet, though my tears dry quickly in the summer sun. I am weeping for him but also for the others, for what he told me, for them. I weep because I cannot understand and there is no way to try, there is nothing more to learn. No one to talk to, no one to explain, no one ever again with whom to share these things. That history ends now, right now, on this hillside. Here on this bluff overlooking a stream, a temple of the earth god and a broken-down hut. It must end and I with it, and as I lose a whole lifetime and go searching for another I am grieving for it all. I am crying out my heartbreak.

It's so unlike me. So unfamiliar. This kind of pain is very new. But I'll survive it; sometime soon it will lessen and then stop, and I'll go back to being brave.

I don't know about my insides. I don't know how they might be. There is blood between my legs that won't stop coming, that is all. A small but steady flow. Not long ago I could feel it in me, I could reach out and touch it with an inner hand, but now I've lost that power. I cannot sense it. So I will have to wait and see.

It doesn't matter, either way. Either way I weep. I just wonder if he knew, somehow, if he guessed but would not say. If it pleased him, if it hurt him. If it figured in his dreams.

Another thing I'll never learn.

A day of waiting can be a terrible ordeal. Of waiting with a certain sort of wounded hope that you can't do without. Of wanting to look ahead, needing to look ahead because the future is transformed—because this is the moment, *this* one, in which you determine the rest of your life—but being unable to, feeling faithless and hollow when you try. Of being caught between what was and what may be.

At first I didn't think he would have any trouble. Aside from the wound he looked much the same; he said it didn't hurt and the medic wasn't worried. I even went so far as to give thanks for my good fortune. I tried to remind myself that it is solved nothing, that it was a temporary reprieve—that it would have helped me had he been killed because then I would have had reason to go and no reason to stay, a rationale at long last for the escape I should have made weeks ago— but still I felt thankful. I didn't want him to die. At a time of frightful danger I found myself to be different, very different, from the Li I'd once known well; I cared more for this attachment than I did for my own safety, more for him than for me. That was the plain fact of it.

And there was also my inertia, the aversion to motion I've accumulated in my months here, plus what was already in my blood. I sensed the fatalistic weight of generations pressing down as I sat by the bed and watched him, that sweet resignation to the barbarities of heaven; I fought it but it was hard. It was so tempting. I felt a gentle form of slumber spreading over me, saturating me, a distant but familiar voice urging me to stop, to surrender and rest. Urging me to go with him in one way or another, to stay with him until his end was made mine, and our fates were joined together.

So I did not believe that he would die. Not at first. Not for hours. It was a new experience for me, this waiting; I had never given much thought to death in the absence of the fact. My parents were taken from me before I ever imagined it was possible, as was my grandmother when I was six. My lack of practice hemmed me in, I was naive and would not question myself; when it seemed he wasn't badly hurt I took this seeming for granted, not knowing or wanting to know that I had reason to be misled.

And the truth wasn't something that I gathered all at once, not a flash of revelation. It crept slowly over me in the night, minute by minute, almost unnoticed until at a certain moment it was there, inside me: the chance that he might die. That he might vanish. That I would be alone again.

Around midnight—hours and hours before the morning, hours before he told me what he told me—he opened his eyes, suddenly, and looked up at me with pity. As if I were the one who'd been stabbed.

"This is the end for me, I'm afraid."

"No."

He watched me without speaking. "It's the end for you too," he said at last. "It's the end for all of us."

When he began his account I was prepared for it, I think. Not for what he told me, not for his death, but for change, for the end of our time together. I felt awful—I felt that a demon was squeezing me, squeezing everything in my skin, collapsing me into a tiny aching ball—but it was the hurt of recognition, of acknowledgment, a hurt I could accept; all my panic was gone. I knew that he believed he was dying, that he was finished, so when he started in I wasn't really taken by surprise.

Funny that you can learn so much about death, just from watching one man go. I am far more experienced now than I was. I wouldn't have guessed it but now I know that a dying person must confess, must disencumber himself and discharge his obligations. A dying person must review his own evil, along with the good, must secure his knowledge of it. Not to alter or explain it, not to lose it, but just to know. This brings comfort and also freedom; it is a lifelong struggle lost.

He was still strong and he insisted on telling me. That is the word: he insisted. His eyes were bright as he talked, and in the lamp's dim light I saw them shine. I tried to stop him, to make him rest, but he waved impatiently and kept on. I tried again with the same result. I was heartened by the vigor of his motions and his speech—for a brief time I was even hopeful again—and it was clear that I could only do him harm by preventing him. He needed to tell me, whatever it was; he was driven, a thing I hadn't seen in him before. So I gave in.

At first I was attentive as he talked of the city; these were things I had often wondered about. I'd been forty miles away and I thought I wanted to know. But when I began to understand what he was actually saying I couldn't listen at all. I told him again to stop but he went ahead. I almost put my fingers in my ears. I knew, I told him, knew as much as I needed, as much as I could stand. I was wrong, he said, I didn't; there was more I had to hear.

Why do it? I asked. Why ruin himself and me and our affection for each other? What was done was done—what possible difference could it make? It happened, he said. It really happened and he was there. That was reason enough.

So I sat and tried to listen.

But something changed as he talked, and the balance slowly shifted. He found it harder to go on, ever harder with each sentence, but I was shocked and then reluctant and then compelled and finally avid, and I wanted to know more. I wanted to know everything. Our paths crossed, our roles changed. He was taken aback; he hadn't meant to share the details. But I pressed and he was forced to.

"Tell me."

"If you want me to."

"Tell me."

"How cruel you are."

His hand was in my lap and I held it between my own. I held it firmly, to give him strength. I was almost giddy with the need to hear it, with anticipation and keen desire; in any other circumstance I would have been embarrassed, I would have held myself back, but at that moment it hardly mattered. I sensed by then that it was a gift, his only legacy, this telling of it, and I had to know—for his sake, for my parents', for the nation's. I'd moved beyond my own concerns.

"Tell me," I said.

"It was bad," he said. "It was very bad. It was worse than you can imagine."

"Then tell me—what was the worst?"

When at last it was over I felt so sorry for him. He was trembling with rage and misery and despair. I got in bed with him then, I held him and cradled his head and kissed him. I whispered comforting things. I didn't want those awful words to be the last he ever spoke to me, or my excited questions my last to him. I said he could forget it now, that I would remember. I urged him to rest. I stroked him and tried to get him to tell me, once more, what he felt about me, how much he cared, and though he said very little it was enough to ease my mind. I had not lost his affection. The sky outside was barely beginning to brighten when I kissed him again and told him I loved him. It was hard for me and I prayed he would not know that but it seemed to make him happy. It was lovely to see him smile at me. A little while later he died in my arms.

In good time I woke the medic. There was courtesy in his look and his nod, in his slow approach to the bed. It was with respect and even tenderness that he arranged Kuroda's head and hands. He is a simple boy but seems also to run deep. He seems to know. He was kind enough to leave us alone while he went to get the lieutenant.

I stood against the wall as Nagai entered the room. To my relief there was no one with him; perhaps he planned to keep me for himself. I assumed—I hoped—that he would have the decency to take me away from Kuroda first, out of sight of him, but perhaps the other room would be far enough. It was still very early; the bugle had not yet sounded. Only the guards would be awake. Perhaps he meant for no one else to be there, I guessed, for no one else to see.

He stood staring at the body for a very long time. Then he looked around the room. At last he noticed me. Our eyes met and held and I did not cast mine down, so I could witness his surprise.

"I'll give you thirty minutes," he said.

I hurried away as fast as I could, without even looking back. I stopped only for my shoes and those I held in my hand. At least one sentry saw me go, but as I had nothing of value with me he decided not to shoot. He didn't know that his captain was dead and was unwilling to risk harming me. I was lucky he didn't shout aloud because the others might have done differently, but this one chose to simply let it happen, to make no fuss. Good riddance, he must have said to himself, let some other man kill her.

As I went I thought of Kuroda. And I thought of what he'd told me. They would burn him, I knew, and send his ashes to Japan. I hated to leave the walls, the floor, the stove I'd loved so well, the pots and the water closet, but my angel did not hold me; he wasn't there anymore. I carried him with me. I carried him as I fled. I held him out in front of me and saw his face in repose, for just a moment, and was eased by that brilliant smile, but then his words came back to hurt me. They came to steal my peace away.

At the base of the hill I paused, looking at the orange glow on the horizon, and tried to decide: west or south? West or south? As I stood his words returned once more and I remembered our grove just a mile to the west, green with *Ailanthus* and bamboo, and the high hill beyond that, and I went the other way.

Twenty thousand. Thirty thousand. My head was spinning, my knees were weak. Even I was overwhelmed. I walked as quickly as I could and as I went I kept hearing it: *Twenty thousand, thirty thousand. Little girls and aged women.* Mothers with babies nursing, mothers with six children behind them, college graduates, prostitutes, shop clerks, students at the missionary schools. Women nine months pregnant. Rich women, poor women, pretty women, plain. Trapped by three soldiers, chased by half a dozen, assaulted by ten or twenty or thirty and left for dead. Mutilated, stabbed or just used and discarded. The playthings of fifty thousand men.

And the rest of it too. He described it very thoroughly, because I made him. He told me about the looting; he told me about the blood. He said at times the sidewalk ran with it. He said he went into one house and emptied his belly straight away, and had to crawl out on his hands and knees, and smashed his head on the door jamb. He said he'd never forgotten the shrieks and the cries. But all that I took for granted, almost, I had known it or assumed it and it was the logical accompaniment, the background to what truly concerned us both. The horror lived mostly in one place for us, it spread from one putrid stain, and he was honest about this; he used the word again and again, repeated it over and over, a word that was clearly strange to his tongue but surely written in his brain. I wondered if he'd ever even spoken it before.

Please tell me, why so much? I asked as I hurried through

the dim morning, my ears and eyes searching the open fields around me. Not just why but why so much, why so much *rape*? It's as if that's what they came for. To dilute our Chinese blood, is that what they wanted? To dirty us for our men? To ruin us, to make us forever joyless and ashamed?

I know it's nothing new. I know. Put any soldiers among women and you'll have rapes, of course you will, you'd be a fool not to expect it. But this was different. This was vast. Hundreds a day, maybe a thousand from what he said, maybe more; most of them doing it, all of them seeing it, none of them stopping it. Not one. Not a single one. Endless, endless horror. Why so long and why so frenzied? And why so many victims? Why?

I almost asked him all of that as he told me his tale; I almost asked him if he knew. But I couldn't push that hard. I did without the final step, perhaps to keep him whole—because I knew I would have him with me, inside me, for the rest of my life—or perhaps to spare myself. I remembered the poem he'd recited for me and felt a chill on my heart, and saw the long years of the future, stretching ahead without him, and decided to be kind.

"Forgive us," he said at one point, having paused to sip some water.

I looked away from him then. It was not for me to do.

The sun had started rising to my left when conscience stopped me. All was silent except the wind. I looked behind and felt regret—I'd made so much progress in so short a time, and the schoolhouse seemed so small—but I could not leave them yet. There were questions unanswered. I turned around and headed back, walking steadily, my pace no faster than before.

As it happened I hadn't far to go. A group of them were coming south on the road. I ran east until they saw me, and when I got close I gave thanks that Yawata was not among them. One raised and aimed his rifle but another pushed it down; I thought for a moment that they hadn't heard, that they were fearful of Kuroda. But then they started toward me and I saw that they knew. They knew very well and they were eager to show me. There was no surprise at the sight of me, no disbelief, only pleasure at their good fortune. I closed my eyes and braced for what I'd always known would come. Then I made myself relax.

They were afraid to fuck me at first. He was dead but still they felt small traces of respect, of duty. They beat me with great joy but were afraid to go further. Finally I tore my tunic open and then they did the rest. They must have thought it was despair that made me give myself to them. They must have thought me insane. They were actually rather gentle with me, I think, compared to what they might have liked; though they used me savagely it could have been much worse. The pain was great but then it ebbed and they were almost organized, even efficient in the way they took their turns, and I found that I could bear it. I was limp and beyond harm. After a minute or so they saw they didn't have to hold me down.

What he saved me from, yes. Betrayal and a debt repaid. I told him they'd come back for me, sooner or later, to add me to the many; I told him and I was right. But it's a blessing he never knew it.

I had very little fear of being killed when they were done. There were flashes of that impulse in the eyes of one or two but they were satiate and exhausted from the beating and the taking, all of them, and it was understood that we'd made an exchange. I had apologized, they felt, for the insults of their commander, and in accepting my abasement they had revenged themselves on him. I had given them a chance they could never have expected—the chance to celebrate his death by raping not just any Chinese woman but his own personal whore, the one they'd cursed and hated so while bound by his restrictions—and they were grateful in their fashion. I don't think they even considered that if I hadn't returned of my own accord I might have gotten clean away; I had come back to pay for liberation, they believed, I had earned it, and that was natural and fair. I had earned it and they would not take it from me. Nor would they free me from my pain.

As they marched off down the road I lay there on my back for a few seconds, one hand in my crotch wet with blood, the other covering my swollen left eye, and tried to feel the child. The sun had at last moved above the horizon. For a week or more I'd felt it, since discovering it was there; I'd felt it every minute of every hour of every day but now I couldn't anymore. I'd even felt it as he told me, as he died and as I ran, but when his soldiers laid their hands on me I lost track of it entirely. I couldn't say it was there but I couldn't say it wasn't; I was numb from the neck downwards, both inside and out. I gathered myself, stood, looked at the blood, pulled on my pants, closed my tunic, tried a step. All this I could do but not feel. I accepted not knowing; muddy water let stand will clear, as the saying goes, and it would come to me in time. I counseled patience to myself and started walking again.

AUTHOR'S NOTE

The author thanks the following for their generous and valued assistance:

Bill Bryant, Haruko Taya Cook, Theodore F. Cook, Ignatius Y. Ding, John W. Dower, Helen Horowitz, Jing-He Liu, Bernice Moy, Judy Perlman, Caroline Rittenhouse, Margaret Bailey Speer, Lois Wheeler Snow, Jeanne Tai, Jim Thomson, Ping Wang, and Yang Zhang.

None of the Chinese place names that appear in this book are spelled according to the Pinyin phonetic standard currently in use for Chinese-to-English translation. Instead they are rendered as they would have been, in English, in 1938. Most appear in the "common English" or "post office" form of that era; some are spelled according to the Wade-Giles phonetic standard in use at the time. In a few instances the English spelling has remained the same since 1938, e.g. Shanghai, or one of several contemporary variants is used because it happens to match the modern Pinyin spelling.